Mr. Darcy's Impulsive Moment

By Zoe Burton

Mr. Darcy's Impulsive Moment

Zoe Burton

Published by Sweet Escapes Press

Early drafts of this story were written and posted on fan fiction forums and on Patreon in 2023 and 2024.

ISBN: 978-1-953138-38-5

Acknowledgements

First, I thank my Savior Jesus Christ for His guidance and for giving me words to write. I love you!

As always, I owe a huge debt of gratitude to my writing buddies, Rose and Leenie. Your input has been invaluable.

I also must thank the fellow writers in my small group, Cheryl and Bill. I'm glad God added you to my circle!

Finally, I offer thanks to my twenty-seven or so followers and Patrons on Patreon. Your support means so much to me, because it tells me my writing is valued. Thank you for the hundredth time, from the bottom of my heart! <3

Chapter 1

Longbourn, Hertfordshire

August 18, 1811

Elizabeth Bennet rubbed beeswax into the last panel on her father's gig then stepped back to admire the shine. "I think that will do it," she said. She looked to her right as Mr. Bennet walked around the corner of the small equipage.

"It is beautiful, my dear." He put his hand on her shoulder. "It makes me proud to know you are able to take care of her if something happens to me."

Elizabeth grinned. "Thank you, Papa."

Bennet squeezed his daughter's shoulder before stepping away. "I think we are done for today. Thank you for your assistance. I will leave you to clean up, but I urge you to do it quickly before your mother realizes where you are."

Elizabeth rolled her eyes. "I will; I promise." She watched her father leave the stables before she began putting her materials away.

Elizabeth was Mr. Bennet's favorite child. They were very much alike. They both enjoyed the written word and read a wide range of subjects. They loved to debate the things they read, as well. Bennet had seen in Lizzy a thirst for learning and had indulged it, educating her as though she were a son and not a daughter. To his delight, she shared a love for more than just reading, writing, and mathematics. She had also inherited his love of anything with wheels.

For as long as Elizabeth could remember, her father had owned the gig. He had once told her that it was a single man's toy and that her mother would prefer him to get rid of it, but Bennet loved it and had restored it himself. That was not a fact he shared with many people. It was unheard of for a gentleman to get his hands dirty, but Elizabeth knew that her Papa reveled in the work. She also knew that the equipage was not part of the estate and that his will left it to her, along with the mare he kept to pull it.

Elizabeth's work on the gig was a tightly-held secret between the two of them. They did their best to hide it from her mother and sisters, with the help of the servants. They were not always successful, which usually led to Elizabeth being more closely monitored for a while by Mrs. Bennet – a circumstance Lizzy hated – but as a rule, they hid it well.

With all her tools and supplies put away, Elizabeth hung her apron up on a peg and crept outside, keeping a sharp eye out for anyone from the house. Seeing no one, she slipped in the back door and through the kitchen, greeting the cook, scullery maid, and housekeeper with a grin and a wave. She turned left into the hallway and tiptoed up the back stairs, knowing the female members of the family were likely in the front parlor at this time of day. She entered her bedchamber, which connected to her elder sister Jane's via a closet, and quickly washed her face and hands, re-pinned her hair, and changed her gown. She was just finishing up when someone knocked on her door.

"Come in!"

Jane slipped into the room, closing the wooden panel behind her and sitting on the bed. "Did you hear Mama's news?"

Elizabeth smiled. "No, I missed it." She winked.

"Oh, Lizzy." Jane laughed. "You are too good at sneaking out to avoid her effusions."

"Mmmm." Elizabeth tried to keep her mien solemn but her lips insisted on twitching. "Perhaps." She broke into a grin when Jane laughed again. "What has made her so happy?"

"She heard from my Aunt Phillips that Netherfield has been let. She said that Mr. Morris brought some papers by Uncle's office to have him copy and that the gentleman will take possession before Michaelmas."

"Indeed?" Elizabeth joined her sister on the bed. "Was she able to describe him?"

Jane shook her head. "No, just that his name begins with a B and he is from the north of England."

"Well," Elizabeth said with a shrug. "Michaelmas is only a few weeks away. Before you know it, we will be meeting this gentleman.

7

Has Mama chosen a wife for him yet?"

"Lizzy!" Jane shook her head but then rolled her eyes and grinned. "I should not encourage you in speaking of your mother this way, but you know she has ... me!"

Elizabeth laughed heartily. "You know why she chose you."

"I do; because I am beautiful." Jane rolled her eyes again and stood. "Hush, now. Instead of talking more about things that are likely never to happen, let us go down to the drawing room. Mama will expect us for tea soon."

"Very well," Elizabeth said as she stood. "Lead on, my fair sister."

Giggling, the two eldest Bennet daughters made their way to the family parlor on the ground floor to await their mother and younger sisters.

Meryton Assembly Rooms, Hertfordshire

October 15, 1811

Fitzwilliam Darcy followed his friends into the local assembly room. He was not looking forward to the coming events of the night, but Charles Bingley, his host, had insisted the entire party attend with him. Since Bingley was new to the area and was considering leasing long-term the estate into which he had recently moved, it behooved him to befriend the neighbors, and since Darcy was not only his friend but also a bit of a mentor, Darcy felt obligated to attend with him. The only thing that made the thought of a room full of strangers who expected him to dance with their daughters acceptable was the sure knowledge that one of the party had a fortune at least as large as his own. *For once, the whispers about money will not be only about mine,* he thought.

Once inside the building, the five of them – Darcy, Bingley, Bingley's sister Louisa Hurst and her husband, Reginald, and Darcy and Bingley's friend, Albert Madison – gave their outerwear to the servant assigned to take them and made their way to the set of double doors behind which an orchestra could be heard tuning up. Bingley and Madison entered first, followed by the Hursts. Darcy brought up the rear.

As he had expected, the entire room fell silent at their entrance. Darcy took a deep breath and stiffened, his entire being wanting nothing more than to melt into the floorboards. He hated being on display. He forced himself to don the mask of indifference that was expected of one of his class, and braced himself for what was surely to come.

At that point, a gentleman of middling years with a touch of gray at his temples approached and bowed to Bingley.

"Welcome to our little assembly, Mr. Bingley!"

Bingley bowed in return. "Thank you, Sir

William. I am happy to be here." He gestured to Madison. "May I introduce you to my friends?"

"Oh, yes! Please do." Sir William Lucas clasped his hands together. Darcy was certain it must be to keep them still, as the gentleman seemed ready to applaud at any moment.

"Beside me is Mr. Albert Madison of Maidstone in Essex. Behind me is my brother, Mr. Reginald Hurst of Greenfriar in Lincolnshire and my sister, Mrs. Hurst, and in the back is Mr. Fitzwilliam Darcy, of Brook Street in London and Pemberley in Derbyshire."

Darcy bowed in greeting, accepting the effusive welcome of the man with nothing more than a nod. Within moments, he found himself following the group as Sir William began to introduce them to the other attendees. He found the exercise tiresome in the extreme. That is, until one face stood out in the crowd.

About halfway down the room, Sir William stopped in front of a group of ladies.

"My eldest daughter you know," he said as he gestured to an older girl standing to the left of the group. "On the right is Mrs. Bennet of Longbourn and her daughters, Miss Jane Bennet and Miss Elizabeth Bennet."

As the ladies curtsied, Darcy was first struck by the fact that Mrs. Bennet and Miss Jane Bennet could have been twins. Both were blonde and beautiful, with big blue eyes. The only difference he could discern between them was the hint of lines fanning out from the mother's eyes. Otherwise, her skin was as smooth and glowing as that of her daughter, and her figure was just as slim. If he had not been introduced, he would not have realized their relationship.

This startling observation was overshadowed, however, when he took in the dark orbs and slightly curled lips of Miss Elizabeth Bennet. Darcy was struck dumb when he looked at her, his heart stopping for a moment before speeding up. His mouth went dry. He bowed, and when he straightened and their eyes met, he felt as though he were falling into a deep well. His face grew hot at the same time he saw her cheeks turn pink. He could not look away, though his ingrained manners were screaming at him that he should. He was startled out of it when he was nudged by one of his friends.

"Darcy is an excellent dancer, though he is not overly fond of the exercise."

Darcy glanced at Bingley before addressing the ladies. "My friend is correct. Dancing is not my favorite activity. However, if Miss Elizabeth Bennet would favor me with her hand, I would be delighted to partner with her."

Elizabeth's light blush deepened, but she smiled prettily and curtseyed. "I would be happy to dance with you, sir. Which set would you like?"

Darcy swallowed, his heart continuing to

race as it had since he first set eyes on her. "The next, if you have it available."

"I am free for the next set. I will keep it for you." Elizabeth kept her gaze trained on his.

The thought that this beautiful, fascinating creature was as entranced by him as he was by her made him wish to take her away somewhere and learn everything there was about her – her thoughts and beliefs, her hopes and dreams, and what it would be like to brush his lips across hers. He swallowed.

"Thank you. I look forward to our dances." He bowed once more and felt his friend pull him along to greet the next family.

As Darcy suffered through the following few minutes of introductions, bowing and murmuring greetings automatically and without thought, his mind was more pleasantly engaged with thoughts of his upcoming dances. He did his best to focus on the conversations his friends were having with the ladies and gentlemen they were meeting, but he failed more often than not. Soon, it was time to claim his dance and he presented himself to Elizabeth once more.

"I believe this is our set." He bowed and held out his hand to her. He was unprepared for the tingle that shot from his palm to his heart the moment her gloved hand touched his. He ceased to breathe momentarily. Swallowing and forcing his eyes from hers, he led her to the dance floor, depositing her on the ladies' side of the line and then taking his place across from her.

As before, once his eyes met those of his partner, Darcy could not look away. When the steps of the dance separated them, as it did regularly throughout the set, he barely was able to smile at the other ladies he turned with. His whole focus was on Elizabeth.

Though Darcy had a difficult time forming thoughts, it appeared his partner did not.

"How do you like Netherfield, Mr. Darcy? I have only been inside it once, but I recall it being very elegantly decorated."

"It is a comfortable house. I find I like it very much. It has a welcoming, cozy feeling to it." Inside, Darcy was amazed that he had managed to speak in such a sensible manner, given the confused plethora of feelings stirring around inside him. "How does it compare to your home? Bingley told me Longbourn is also very nice."

"I believe Longbourn is quite lovely, but I am biased, I fear."

Elizabeth laughed, and the warm, rich sound made him want to kiss her.

"The rooms are well-appointed, I think, and in the family quarters, they are quite comfortably furnished. The public rooms are a little fussy, but my mother insists they must be so for company. It would not do for anyone to think we were lesser than we are." She rolled her eyes.

Darcy chuckled. "Indeed," he said. "I recall my mother saying something similar at some point."

Elizabeth tilted her head to look up at him as they promenaded down the line. "She does not do so now?"

Darcy shook his head, a pang hitting his heart. "My mother passed away when I was young."

Elizabeth's free hand came up to cover her mouth. "Oh! I am so sorry!"

Darcy shrugged. "You could not have known. All is well."

"Thank you, sir. You are most kind and forgiving." She squeezed his hand, which she had been holding as part of the dance. "What about your father? Is he still with you?"

"Sadly, no. He joined my mother four or five years ago. There is only me and my younger sister now, along with some aunts, uncles, and cousins on both my parents' sides of the family."

"How awful for you to have lost both parents. I cannot imagine losing even one." Elizabeth stepped back to her side and clapped along with the music. "How old is your sister?"

"She is more than ten years my junior. She is in town with her companion, taking advantage of the masters."

"She must have been very young when your parents passed away. Have you raised her, then?"

14

"I have." He fell silent for a moment. "I have not always been the best parent in the world. I have failed spectacularly on many occasions."

"I cannot imagine being guardian to one of my sisters. I admire that you have managed so far. Is she difficult?" Elizabeth glanced down the line to where two younger girls were laughing loudly as they danced, and then turned her attention back to Darcy. "My own sisters, except for Jane and possibly Mary, are a handful. The youngest are seventeen and fifteen. I could often be challenging at their ages, so I would imagine such behavior would be universal at that time of life."

"Georgiana can be rather emotional at times, but she is generally well-behaved and quiet. She is shy and eager to please, which must, in part, explain ..." Darcy trailed off, suddenly realizing that he was about to tell a total stranger the story of his sister's recent broken heart. He was silent for a few minutes as they applauded the orchestra as one song ended and they waited for the next. Thankfully, this last dance of the set was one that allowed for more conversation.

Elizabeth had not spoken, content, it seemed, to allow Darcy to think about what to say next. She watched him, smiling when he caught her eye.

"All I can say is, my sister is not generally one to cause a scene. She does not like being the center of attention. However, when it is just the two of us at home, she is more than capable of expressing her displeasure." One corner of Darcy's lips lifted as he noted his partner's eyes twinkling.

"That is something every female is capable of, I believe." Her brow lifted.

Darcy laughed out loud. "Indeed." He held out his arm for her to rest her hand on as they promenaded down the line.

The remainder of their dance was spent in similar conversation, speaking about their families and homes. Darcy was disappointed when the set ended and he had to return Elizabeth to her mother's side. He bowed deeply to her and reluctantly walked away. For the rest of the evening, he remained along the edge of the dance floor, though he did perform a set with his host's sister once. Even then, his attention was more on Elizabeth than it was Louisa.

Chapter 2

Later that night, after the party returned to Netherfield, Darcy, Bingley, Hurst, and Madison enjoyed a nightcap in Bingley's study.

"Well, gentlemen, what did you think? Darcy, have either you or Madison attended a country assembly before?" Bingley handed each man a glass of port.

"I have a few times at home. My mother is quite fond of them and purchases a ticket every year for the assembly hall in the nearby town." Madison sipped his wine. "They are quite enjoyable if one likes to dance."

"That they are." Bingley grinned. "Darcy, what about you?"

"I confess to attending one in the village of Kympton once, but as you know, dancing is not one of my preferred activities unless I am particularly acquainted with my partner. I knew none of the ladies at that assembly and so did not enjoy the experience." He set his glass on the small table at his elbow. "I never repeated it. Tonight is only my second time appearing at such an affair."

"You seemed to enjoy yourself this time." Hurst leaned back into his chair and settled himself comfortably. "You danced with a stranger."

Darcy felt himself flush. "I did." He clamped his lips shut. He refused to discuss it, especially since he had not had time to process his actions himself.

"I did, as well." Madison raised his brows. "It is to be expected."

Bingley snorted. "Well, Darcy has never exerted himself to do so before now at any ball, including his aunt's annual Christmas ball. I simply find it interesting that we come to the country, to a place he has never been before, and he immediately asks a lady he has never met in his life to dance with him." He lifted his glass. "It is most perplexing." He took a sip.

Darcy shrugged. "I have no explanation. It seemed like the proper thing to do at the time." He eyed his friend for a second, deciding to make an attempt at turning the conversation. "You did as you usually do and found the most stunning blonde in the room to dance with."

Bingley grinned. "Is she not the most beautiful thing you have ever beheld?"

Darcy did not agree, but chose to say nothing.

"She is the mirror image of her mother." Hurst looked around at the other gentlemen. "Did you notice that?"

Darcy nodded, just as the others did. "I did see it. It was amazing."

"If you did not know they were mother and daughter, they could be taken as sisters. I do not know if I have ever witnessed a matron who looked as well as Mrs. Bennet." Madison shook his head. "I wonder if Mr. Bennet is the jealous sort. If my wife looked that good after all those children, I would never leave her side for fear of someone enticing her away."

Hurst lifted his glass to his lips. "Her speech, though." He shivered. "You may not have heard it, as it was while you and Darcy were dancing, but she was loud and brash. She gossiped a great deal, including about Bingley and Miss Bennet."

Bingley laughed. "I did notice, when I returned Miss Bennet to her side, that Mrs. Bennet liked the thought of me as a son-in-law."

A crease split Darcy's brow. "How can you laugh at that? She has you married off already to her daughter, as though you were her possession." It was his turn to shiver. He uncrossed his legs and then crossed them the other way. "I cannot imagine her as my mother-in-law."

Madison tilted his head and appeared to examine Darcy. "Have you never met Viscountess Tansley's mother? Bird-witted, that one is, and with no concept of proper speech." He shrugged. "I suppose being a marchioness means she does not have to, but I confess to being surprised she is not censured by the *ton* sometimes."

Darcy shifted uncomfortably again. "I have met her, once, and I do recall that she is a bit buffle-headed. I suppose many families have relations of whom they are not proud."

The gentlemen fell silent and Darcy looked

19

at Bingley, who had blushed and was staring into his glass with a forlorn look on his face. Not long after this, the four of them said good night and retired to their rooms.

~~~***~~~

The next morning, Darcy and Bingley rode out together after breakfast. Madison and Hurst stayed behind to play billiards, while Louisa made a few visits to neighborhood ladies.

Darcy waited until they were out of earshot of the stables before he began speaking. "I apologize if I made you uncomfortable last night when I made that comment about relations and not being proud of them."

"Thank you, but really, there is no need. The situation happened and nothing can be done about it." Bingley shrugged. "Caroline made the choices she did and now she must bear the consequences. Literally."

"I would imagine it would be painful to have to send your sister away like that." Darcy's thoughts were filled with his own dear sister and what might have happened just two months ago, had he not decided to drop in on her at her lodgings in Ramsgate. "It would have torn me apart to banish Georgiana."

Bingley was quiet for a moment. "It was painful. My sister is not the easiest person to live with, I grant you." He sighed and shook his head. "Part of me cannot believe that she would have allowed herself to be seduced by anyone. She has always been the shrewdest female I have ever known, and yet, she fell for a lying cad."

It was Darcy's turn to be quiet for a moment. "How is her pregnancy going?"

"Well, I guess. Louisa writes to her every week and receives letters in return. She tells me the morning sickness is over and that Caroline has had to order some new gowns. She has felt the quickening and is getting bigger every day. Our aunt visits twice a week, but she never sees any of our other relatives. She goes nowhere and sees no one and that grates on her. I do not know how she will last until the birth."

"Will she keep the child or give it up?"

Bingley shrugged again. "I do not know. She says she is looking for a family to take it so she can move back to London, but the fact is, her life as she knew it is over. Even if she were to return to town, her reputation is ruined. She will not be invited anywhere, especially not to the homes of the people she used to be friendly with. Maybe she should raise the child herself, but even that is fraught with dangers. She is living respectably enough. Her fortune is more than enough to provide them a good, safe home and plenty of servants. She should not have to worry about men thinking they can accost her in her own house."

"Some will, regardless."

Bingley's shoulders fell. "I know." He looked

at his friend. "I have never been in such a difficult place. I was supposed to take care of her, but my father always insisted we pay the natural consequences of our actions. So, that is what I have done with Caroline. I have made her face this alone as all of society seems to dictate. I feel as though I have failed her, but she made her choices."

"I wish I knew how to help you. I truly do. I will continue to pray for Caroline and for you."

"Thank you. You are an excellent friend, Darcy." Bingley looked around at the field they were crossing. "I would like to get to know Miss Bennet better. I am afraid, though. What if the feelings I have for her are love, or even are not but turn into it, and she rejects me because of my sister? Others have, as you are aware."

"All I know to say is to take your time and make certain you understand her character before you allow yourself to become too attached. Even then, rejection is possible." Darcy lifted a shoulder. "I suppose you could pretend you do not have a sister and never mention it, but I do not think that would be honest."

"No." Bingley straightened his shoulders. "I will do as you suggest and take my time to learn what manner of person she is. If I feel, in the end, that she will not reject me for my sister's folly, I will know how to act, and if I think she will reject a connection to me, I will move on. My days of impulsivity must, I fear, be over." He sighed. "Thanks to Caroline."

Darcy did not reply, as they had reached a long stretch of road that ran along the edge of the Netherfield property. Instead, he kicked Apollo into motion, silently challenging his friend to a race.

Longbourn

October 16, 1811

The day after the assembly found the Bennet ladies at home, lounging about the drawing room and working on various projects. Jane and Elizabeth were embroidering, Mary was writing out extracts from her favorite book of sermons, Kitty and Lydia were remaking bonnets, and Mrs. Bennet was chattering away at each of her girls in turn.

The housekeeper interrupted their quiet afternoon by announcing visitors.

"Lady Lucas, Miss Lucas, and Miss Maria Lucas to see you, ma'am."

The Bennets jumped up from their pursuits to curtsey to their friends.

"What a wonderful surprise! We did not hear you come into the yard." Mrs. Bennet waved them in. "Come and sit a while."

"We walked today. The weather is fine and I thought it would do us good." Lady Lucas joined her hostess in front of the sofa. Charlotte moved to sit with Elizabeth, Jane, and

23

Mary at their table, and Maria rushed to where Lydia and Kitty were located near the window on the other wall.

"It is a beautiful day." Mrs. Bennet turned to the housekeeper. "We will have tea, and tell Cook to include some of the cake she made this morning."

Mrs. Hill curtseyed. "Very good, ma'am." She left the room again.

"Well." Mrs. Bennet sank onto the sofa beside her friend. "What did you think of the assembly last night? Did you see how taken Mr. Bingley was with Jane?"

Lady Lucas nodded. "I did." She glanced across the room at her eldest daughter and then leaned closer to her hostess. "Mr. Madison did the same with my Charlotte, though she will hear nothing of an attachment."

"Why ever not?" Mrs. Bennet turned with wide eyes toward the table where her neighbor's daughter sat. "Does she not wish to marry?"

"Oh, she does. Or at least, I hope she does." Lady Lucas sat back. "I suspect she is afraid of putting any attachment that might happen in peril, or worse, being the cause of it not forming at all."

Mrs. Bennet looked doubtful for a moment, but could think of nothing to say to refute it. "Well," she finally said, "if she does not want him, perhaps he would do for Mary." She looked across the room to where her middle daughter sat wearing somber colors and writing out a sermon and bit her lip. "Or, maybe Lydia." She smiled in the direction of her favorite child for a moment before turning her attention back to her friend.

Across the room, Elizabeth observed her mother's conversation with a raised brow. She turned to Charlotte.

"I did notice that Mr. Madison seemed to enjoy your company above all others."

Charlotte blushed. "I am sure he was simply being kind."

Jane tilted her head and watched the older girl's eyes look toward the floor. "He does seem to be very kind, but his attention was often drawn toward you, Charlotte, even when he was dancing with other young ladies. I suspect your mother is correct and that you have caught yourself a suitor."

Charlotte shifted in her chair. "I suppose time will tell."

"What do you know about him?" Elizabeth picked up the hoop with her work in it and pushed the needle through the fabric, though her gaze frequently returned to her friend.

Charlotte shrugged. "He is six and twenty – nearly seven and twenty – and is master of his estate in Essex. He has three younger sisters, who are currently at home with their mother."

Elizabeth's eyes grew wide. "It sounds as though you discovered quite a bit about him while you danced."

Charlotte's blush deepened. "He visited Lucas Lodge with Mr. Bingley and Mr. Darcy not long after they took up residence at Netherfield. I was called upon to deliver a tea tray to them in Father's study and overheard the information."

"So you were introduced before the assembly, then." Jane smiled. "How fortuitous. Did he speak to you at that time?"

Charlotte rolled her eyes. "He did, briefly. However, I did not linger. I delivered the tray, suffered through my father's introductions, and left the room."

"You clearly made an impression on him. He could not take his eyes off you all night." Elizabeth grinned when her friend glared at her, then looked back down at her needlework.

"Did you learn anything else about the gentlemen?" Mary looked up from her writing. "What?"

Elizabeth had looked at her next younger sister in surprise when she asked her question. Now she noticed that Jane and Charlotte had done the same. "I am astonished that you asked that particular question is all." She turned her eyes back to their guest. "But it is an excellent one and I hope you have a reply." She raised a brow.

"I do, actually." Charlotte paused and raised her own brow before she continued. "Mr. Madison's estate is called Maidstone and his income is about ten thousand pounds per annum. Mr. Bingley is from trade; his father owned several mills in Yorkshire and left him a hefty fortune. He plans at some point to purchase an estate, and views leasing Netherfield as a first step in that direction. His income is about five thousand pounds per annum. Mr. Darcy is from Derbyshire, is about the same age and income as Mr. Madison, and also owns his estate."

Elizabeth's jaw dropped as her friend spoke. "You overheard all this in the space of a couple minutes?"

"Of course not!" Charlotte laughed. "You know that my father loves to gossip. Some of this he heard from the gentlemen themselves and the rest he got from your uncle." She shrugged. "He was eager to share it with someone and Mama and I were the closest people."

Elizabeth chuckled. "Sir William does enjoy a good story, does he not?"

Charlotte rolled her eyes. "He does!"

A crease formed between Mary's brows. "Did you learn anything of their character?"

Charlotte shook her head. "Not really. I can tell you that Mr. Bingley is friendly, Mr. Darcy is somber and quiet, and Mr. Madison is somewhere in between the two."

"We will have to be in their company to learn more, I think." Elizabeth rested her hand on Mary's arm. "I, for one, will enjoy getting to know all of them, and Mrs. Hurst."

"Yes." Jane nodded. "She seemed to be a

very nice person." She paused. "I almost got the feeling that she was worried or somehow …" She huffed, shrugging her shoulders. "I do not know … ashamed, almost." She shook her head. "Ignore me. I do not know what I am speaking about."

"No, I got the same feeling. Almost as though she were deeply grateful that we would speak to her." Elizabeth looked over her sister's shoulder, becoming lost in thought. "I wonder why?"

"I do not know, but I am happy to make a new friend, so I hope she is as kind in the future as she was last night." Charlotte suddenly grinned. "Now that we are finished examining my evening, what about you two, Jane and Eliza? It seems as though both of you were objects of attraction to Mr. Bingley and his friends, as well."

Elizabeth and her sister blushed. The rest of the Lucases' visit was spent teasing the eldest Bennets about certain of the newcomers to the area.

Chapter 3

Netherfield Park

October 18, 1811

Darcy followed his friends as they made their way through one of the far fields at the back of the Netherfield estate. The steward, Mr. Frary, was in the lead, and several servants trailed behind, carrying the firearms the gentlemen would need. Walking alongside Darcy was a local landowner named Mr. Long, and off to his other side were Mr. Bennet, Mr. Goulding, and Sir William Lucas.

"So you are from Derbyshire, Mr. Darcy?"

Mr. Long's question brought Darcy out of his contemplations. "I am. My estate is called Pemberley."

"I have heard of the beauties of that area. Mrs. Long would like to travel there one day. Her sister has visited The Peaks and is full of stories of their grandeur and magnificence."

"If you get the opportunity, you should do as your wife wishes. It would be an unforgettable experience. My estate is a little south of The Peaks, but my family has a small cottage along the southern edge of the district. We spent part of every summer there when I was growing up."

"You have decided me, sir. I will plan a trip

for next year. Perhaps I will surprise Mrs. Long with it."

The conversation was interrupted when the group stopped and some birds were flushed out for them to shoot. A short while later, when they moved to a new location a short distance away, Darcy found himself next to Mr. Long once more. This time, Bennet, Sir William, and Mr. Goulding were far enough away that they could not hear his conversation. He was glad of it, for he hoped to glean some information about the Bennet family, and Elizabeth in particular.

"You seemed to enjoy our little assembly this past Tuesday." The older man glanced at him as he handed his firearm to a servant. "I heard my wife speaking admiringly of you and your friends the next day."

Darcy blushed. "It was a delightful gathering." He shrugged. "I do not like to be on display, and I dislike dancing unless I am particularly acquainted with my partner, but I found the ladies in attendance to be very pleasing."

"You danced with Miss Elizabeth Bennet, did you not?" Mr. Long looked from Darcy to the servant, who was now reloading his gun.

"I did." Darcy felt heat under his collar. "She is an excellent dancer."

"That she is. All of the Bennet girls are. Their mother has made sure of it." Mr. Long paused, taking his weapon in hand and lifting it toward the sky to look down the barrel. "Miss Elizabeth has a sharp wit." He nodded toward Bennet as he lowered the gun to his side. "I believe her father took a specific interest in her education, though he encouraged all of them to learn. He is a bit indolent, though, and I do not believe he pushed the two youngest."

Darcy nodded. "Miss Elizabeth told me she loves to read."

"Oh yes. Always has her nose in a book." Long tipped his head in the direction of Longbourn. "She likes to walk her father's estate and often takes one with her. It is not uncommon to find her on Oakham Mount, reading." He paused. "It is a shame her portion is so small. She will find it difficult to find a husband to match her for wit and intelligence."

Their conversation was once again interrupted, and this time, they never had an opportunity to pick it up again.

Later that day, as Darcy bathed in his dressing room in preparation for dinner, he reflected on what he had learned. It was nothing more than he expected, if he were honest. Elizabeth Bennet had been a charming and witty companion during their set. She had displayed a keen intelligence that he would like to more deeply explore. However, he was uncertain if he should. Mr. Long had indicated that her dowry was small. He had plenty of money, of course, so that would not be a problem too big to overcome. He decided he was not concerned about that.

What did give him pause was his reaction to her the night of the assembly. He had spent days alternately avoiding the contemplation of it and thinking about it incessantly.

As Darcy had indicated to Mr. Long, he was not fond of dancing, as a rule. He also never danced with anyone who was not a member of his own party. And yet, he had asked a complete and total stranger for her hand for a set. *What was I thinking?* He shook his head in wonder at his actions. Days later and all he could say was that he was bewitched by her eyes. He looked into the mirror in his dressing room and spoke to his reflection.

"I do not know what I was thinking or why I asked her to dance, but it feels absolutely right – as though we were meant to be together, as though she belongs to me and I to her. I cannot explain it. I will, however, be cautious and learn more about her before I make any move toward courting her. I must learn more of her before I do aught else."

~~~***~~~

The next evening, Darcy had the opportunity to do just that. The Netherfield party had been invited to dine at Haye Park, the home of Mr. and Mrs. Long. By now, Darcy had met and spoken to nearly all the gentlemen in the area and his discomfort in the presence of strangers was not as strong, except, of course, for the ladies. Of them, he was still pretty much unacquainted with most.

To his delight, Elizabeth and her family were in attendance at the party. He would be able to observe her, and perhaps even speak with her again. He wished to know if she was truly as charming as he had thought her earlier in the week, or if he had somehow elevated her in his mind to a level she could not attain.

Darcy was not seated near the object of his attraction at dinner. The situation was, he felt, unfortunate. However, he was able to observe her interactions with others and her reactions to them. He caught her eye once, to his delight. His breath caught in his chest when her fine, dark orbs sparkled at him and her lips lifted into a delightful smile. He sighed to himself. Then, his attention was caught by the lady seated next to him and the moment was lost. *All is well,* he thought. *I will be able to speak with her later in the evening.*

Eventually, the meal ended and the sexes separated. Darcy followed Elizabeth with his eyes as she departed the dining room with her sisters. Thankfully, the parting was not long and almost before he knew it, he was following his host into the drawing room.

The gentlemen scattered throughout the chamber, eager to see the ladies again. One of the younger girls was at the pianoforte, playing a quiet tune while the guests chatted.

Darcy began to make a circuit of the room, in part to keep himself occupied and in part to bring himself closer to Elizabeth. He was stopped part way around by a pair of very young ladies who looked very similar.

"You are a rather handsome gentleman, are you not?" The darker-haired girl attached herself to his arm, looking up at him and fluttering her lashes. "Do you not think he and I look very well together, Kitty?"

The other girl, slightly taller and with lighter hair, giggled. "Indeed you do, Lydia. You make a handsome couple."

Darcy had stiffened the second he was touched. He had too much experience with ladies of the *ton* to take for granted that the girls' intent was not malicious. He was shocked at their forwardness with a gentleman who was, in essence, a stranger to them. A scowl marred his features as he addressed them.

"Pardon me. I have not given you leave to behave so familiarly with me."

He was not certain his words had even entered the girls' ears, for just as he finished speaking, they darted away from him, approaching an officer of the militia that was stationed outside of Meryton and stealing his sword. Darcy huffed as he watched them run down the room with it.

"Those two are a handful." Bingley stepped closer, shaking his head at the young ladies' antics, his lips twisted into a smirk.

"Indeed." Darcy's brow was creased to match his frown. "They are wild and unchecked and belong in the schoolroom. I wonder at their being allowed out in public to behave in such a manner. I was about to say just that to them when they let go of me and decided to chase that officer."

Bingley tipped his head in the direction of Jane and Elizabeth. "It seems their older sisters are taking them in hand."

Darcy searched the other end of the room and, seeing that his friend was correct, allowed his affront to fade somewhat. The sight of Elizabeth speaking to her sister distracted him from further contemplation of the event. He stared at her, wishing it was he to whom she was speaking, even if it meant she was berating him for an offense. He sighed to himself.

Bingley's voice drew him out of his thoughts. "Is she not the most beautiful creature you have ever beheld?"

Darcy's head whipped toward his friend as jealousy ripped through him. "Who?"

Bingley's brows rose. "Why, Miss Bennet, of course."

"Oh." Darcy cleared his throat. "She is beautiful, but she smiles too much. Her sister, on the other hand ..." His voice trailed off as his eyes returned to gaze upon the fascinating brunette.

"Miss Bennet smiles too much but Miss Elizabeth does not? I wonder sometimes at your logic." Bingley nudged Darcy with his elbow and then, when he had gained his attention, waved a hand in the direction of the ladies. "Have you seen how often *she* does the same? If I did not have personal knowledge of your superior marks at University, I would have to believe you have lost your senses."

Darcy was suddenly hot all over. He cleared his throat. "Well." He could not think of anything to say and so remained silent.

"Come. Let us go and speak to them while we have the opportunity to do so. I am eager to learn more of them and propriety has kept us apart long enough." Bingley grabbed Darcy's arm and headed off to the other end of the chamber. Within seconds, they were standing in front of Jane and Elizabeth.

"Good evening." Bingley bowed to them, and Darcy followed suit, murmuring his own greeting.

"Good evening." Jane and Elizabeth spoke – and curtseyed – in unison.

Darcy found their performance charming. When the younger of the two met his eyes, he felt his heart begin to pound.

"Darcy and I were just admiring how well you handled your younger sisters."

The ladies glanced at each other and blushed. "They are rather high-spirited and often require reminders of what is expected from them." Elizabeth glanced to her side, where Lydia was chattering away with Maria Lucas.

"They do not always listen to us, sadly."

Jane smiled. "They mean no harm with their liveliness, I am sure. They are full young and have yet to learn to temper themselves. I am certain that our instruction will one day come to their minds in such a situation and then they will follow it."

Darcy noticed Elizabeth's eyes begin to roll and bit down on his lower lip to keep from laughing out loud. He cleared his throat. "Would you like to take a turn about the room, Miss Elizabeth?"

Though she blushed prettily, Elizabeth instantly agreed. She tucked her hand under Darcy's elbow and they began to wend their way through the crowd and the furniture, slowly promenading up and down the length of the chamber. He searched his mind for something to say. His mouth had gone dry the moment she had touched him. He swallowed and took a deep breath.

"What say you of books?" He cringed at the inane topic his mind had chosen.

"I say books are wonderful. I love to read and will devour every tome I can get my hands on." She peeked up at him. Her smile made his lips curl up, as well.

"I would have to agree with you. Do you have a favorite topic to read about? Do you prefer histories to crop rotation?"

Elizabeth laughed, and Darcy felt the warm sound fill his insides.

"I confess that of those two, I much prefer histories. The books on crop rotation held my interest but not enough that I would wish to peruse them twice."

"Ah." Darcy smirked. "I had feared that was so. I find nothing more invigorating than a good treatise on farming." He winked and then, when Elizabeth laughed again, grinned at her.

"Well, then. Perhaps we should narrow our discussion to fiction versus those works that are not."

Darcy chuckled. "I think you are correct. Therefore, I will ask my question again, altering it appropriately. Do you prefer dramatized stories such as Shakespeare's works, or does your taste run to true histories? Do you enjoy fiction, as in poetry and novels? Which do you prefer, histories or fiction?"

"There you go." Elizabeth squeezed his arm. "A well-worded inquiry." She laughed. "I love history, though not the dry facts. Instead, I like to read about the more personal aspects of the things that have happened in our past. For example, what did the citizenry have to go through during the Hundred Years' War? What was life like in that time period? Was Henry the Eighth as bad as everyone says he was? What was it like to be a soldier two centuries ago? What was it like to be a gentleman's daughter, or a washerwoman?" She shrugged. "I am curious about things that are not the focus of most histories, but I enjoy reading what is available."

"I had not given much thought to those topics, but now that you mention it, I would find such study interesting, as well. I shall have to search for books on those topics to add to my libraries." Darcy guided Elizabeth around a large group as he thought of what else he might ask her. He decided that books were a good topic to stick to. "Do you have a favorite author?"

"I have several. I enjoy Cowper's poetry and Shakespeare's comedies, and I prefer Fanny Burney's works to those of Ann Radcliffe. There are others, of course, but I could go on and on for hours and that would be rude." She laughed, bringing her hand up over her mouth.

Darcy laughed with her. "Shakespeare is a favorite of mine, as well, though I prefer his histories, and I avoid novels whenever I can."

"You cannot always eschew them?" Elizabeth tilted her head and looked up at him with a raised brow.

"Not always, no." He shook his head. "I insist upon approving all of my sister's reading material, which means that I often must read this novel or that one because she has requested it."

"I think it is wise of you to do so." She glanced in the direction of her youngest sisters, who had stopped running about the room but were now flirting outrageously with a group of red-coated gentlemen in the corner. "Would that every parent or guardian did the same."

Further conversation was interrupted at that point when one of her sisters pulled Elizabeth away and the family left the gathering, surprisingly being the first to leave.

Chapter 4

The two days since the dinner at Haye Park had not been easy for the residents of Longbourn. Mrs. Bennet had overheard Darcy's harsh words about her favorite daughter and was displeased by what she viewed as that gentleman's rudeness.

"I do not understand what a kind and obliging gentleman like Mr. Bingley sees in a rude and ill-mannered person like Mr. Darcy. The nerve of the man, insinuating that my dearest Lydia is childish! He called her wild!" Mrs. Bennet repeated the same refrain to everyone who would listen. When Elizabeth, her least favorite daughter, tried to explain how Darcy might feel as he did, the matron refused to hear her. "You would do well to stay away from him, Miss Lizzy. Do not think I did not notice you speaking to him last night. I will not have it."

Knowing that it was nearly impossible to change her mother's mind when the woman had it set on something, Elizabeth desisted. *I suppose it matters not,* she thought. *I admire him greatly but I have nothing to offer a man such as he.* She sighed. *Would that things were different.* Knowing they were not and that pining after something she could not have would lead to melancholy, something she was not made for, she put it out of her mind the best she could and focused on what was before her.

Later that day, Mrs. Hill announced a visitor.

"Mrs. Hurst to see you, ma'am."

The Bennet ladies rose as Louisa entered and curtseyed.

"Welcome to Longbourn, Mrs. Hurst. Do come in. Hill, a tea tray, if you please."

Elizabeth heard her mother's words but was more focused on their visitor. Louisa displayed a similar tentative timidity to the one she had the previous evening.

Mrs. Bennet gestured to a chair nearby. "Please be seated. It is so good of you to come visit us here."

Elizabeth did her best not to roll her eyes. She was quite sure her mother was more interested in promoting Jane to Mrs. Hurst's brother than she was in actually befriending the woman herself.

"Thank you for having me." Louisa perched on the edge of the chair. She smiled at the ladies around her. "You have a very nice home. It exudes comfort and warmth."

Mrs. Bennet looked around and returned her guest's smile. "Thank you. It has been an age since I decorated, but it has worn well, I think."

"That points to your wisdom in choosing quality materials." Louisa fidgeted with her bracelets. It seemed to Elizabeth that she did this without thought.

Mrs. Bennet preened at her guest's compliment. "I purchased the best I could find and I am happy I did. Five daughters can be rather rough on the furnishings."

Louisa chuckled. "I should imagine so." She looked around at the aforementioned girls. "I hope to have several children myself one day so that I can say the same."

Elizabeth and her sisters laughed with their guest and jumped into the conversation. Mrs. Bennet made sure to steer it towards the gentlemen at Netherfield, especially Mr. Bingley. Eventually, the other girls grew tired of hearing of him and began asking about Mr. Darcy and Mr. Madison.

"My brother has gone out with his friends today for some sport, and Mr. Hurst went with them, so I thought it the perfect time to make some calls."

"We are so glad you did." Jane leaned toward Louisa. "We do enjoy visitors."

"We do!" Lydia fairly bounced in her seat. "You must tell us more of your brother's friends."

Louisa's brows rose and fell. "I know very little of them, to be honest. I am ashamed to admit that, until recently, I paid little attention to the friends of my siblings." She blushed and looked down, biting her lip.

Elizabeth tilted her head. Her brow creased as she watched her guest. "Do you have other brothers, then?"

Louisa's countenance became a deeper

shade of red. "No, I have a sister. She is away for a time, visiting our relations in the north. We have a maiden aunt who took a fall recently, and Caroline went up to assist her as she recovers."

"What a nice thing for her to do!" Elizabeth smiled. "Have they always been close?"

Louisa shook her head. "Not always, but the timing was right, as my sister is recovering from an illness herself, and so off she went."

Elizabeth sat back. "It was still a very nice thing to do, especially since she herself was recently ill."

Lydia apparently had enough of listening to a conversation about a woman she had never met, because she suddenly burst out with a question. "What about the other gentlemen? I think Mr. Madison is sweet on our friend Charlotte."

Louisa seemed relieved to have the subject changed, for she heartily embraced the new topic of conversation. "Charlotte is Miss Lucas?" When the Bennet ladies confirmed that fact, she continued. "He did mention that he enjoyed his dances and conversations with her. My brother has said he has never seen him pay so much attention to a lady before, so you may be correct."

Kitty looked up from her place at the table nearby, where she had been sketching while she listened. "I understand he is from Essex?"

Louisa accepted a cup of tea from Jane, who was serving while her mother poured. "I believe so. His father passed away at about the same time as Mr. Darcy's did. Their circumstances are very similar, except Mr. Darcy has only one sister and no parents at all."

"Charlotte heard from her father that they are wealthy gentlemen." Lydia tucked a foot under her.

To Elizabeth, Louisa looked uncomfortable again. "Yes," she replied hesitantly. She shrugged. "They do travel in the highest circles."

"Then, if our friend were to marry Mr. Madison, she would be very well set." Elizabeth sat back a little with a satisfied smile. "She deserves it. She also deserves love, and if her recent behavior is any indication, I think she is well on her way to being so."

Lydia fell back into her chair, feigning a swoon. "I hope a rich man falls in love with me."

Everyone laughed at her antics and the conversation moved on. Soon, it was time for Louisa's visit to end. They said goodbye with promises by the Bennets to visit her at Netherfield soon.

After their guest was gone and the ladies had separated to their own pursuits, Elizabeth took a book and wandered out to the garden, to the folly in the center of the little wilderness area at the far end of the rose beds. She settled in there and opened her book but did not actually read. Instead, she

45

pondered what Louisa had said about Mr. Darcy. It really was nothing she did not already know, though to have his income confirmed was at the same time comforting and disheartening. *I know he will look elsewhere for marriage, no matter how well he might like me,* she thought with a sigh. *I need to forget these silly thoughts that keep entering my head about him.* With another sigh, she allowed herself to mourn the loss of a love she had not really had, and when she was certain she could keep herself under good regulation, she went back into the house.

Longbourn

October 23, 1811

Elizabeth watched her mother scurry about checking the tables for the card party they were hosting that night. She shook her head. Mrs. Hill knew what she was about and her mother was aware of it, but it did not stop her from allowing her nerves to get the best of her.

Hoping to avoid more of Mrs. Bennet's dramatics, Elizabeth escaped to the gardens, where Jane was cutting flowers to add to the table.

"Finally made your escape, did you?" Jane's brow rose as she cut the thorns off a rose.

Elizabeth rolled her eyes. "I did. I feared becoming ensnared into doing something to help prepare."

Jane laughed. "As I have?"

Elizabeth shook her head but could not prevent a giggle escaping. "Exactly. But, at least this is something you enjoy."

"I do like it. I find it relaxing." Jane gestured with the scissors. "It is so quiet and peaceful out here that I am able to order my thoughts quite nicely."

"Yes," Elizabeth replied. "I agree. Certainly, trying to make sense of anything in the house is nearly impossible with the noise and arguing."

Jane tilted her head. "We have a large family. Noise is to be expected."

"We have a boisterous family." Elizabeth raised a brow as she corrected her sister. "There are many families much larger than ours with quieter houses."

"I concede your point. Our sisters and mother are rather expressive and that can make for a lively home."

"Oh, Jane. You could make a sow who has wallowed in cow droppings seem as pure as snow." Elizabeth rolled her eyes as she laughed. "Let me carry that for you," she said as she took the basket.

"I only say what I think." Jane's lips lifted in her typical serene smile.

Elizabeth grinned. "I know. That is why everyone loves you so much."

Hearing her name, she turned to see Mr. Bennet walking in her direction. "Yes, Father?"

"Your mother finds that she needs a few last-minute items from the grocer in Meryton. I have told her you will go into town for them in her stead. I have had the gig hitched up." He took the basket Elizabeth was holding. "Go in and get the list. By the time you are ready to go, the groom will have brought it around to the door for you." He paused, laying one hand on her shoulder. "I know you will benefit from the exercise of driving. Be careful taking the turn before Netherfield."

"I will, Papa. Thank you."

Elizabeth hurried into the house. In short order, she had her mother's shopping list and was climbing into the equipage. With a nod to the groom who handed her up, she gathered the reins and slapped them on Gracie's back. Soon, the gates that closed off the home's driveway were flying past her. She grinned when she gained the open road, urging the mare to pick up speed.

Elizabeth loved the feel of the wind against her face and the pull of the animal against the reins. She loved going fast and there were few in the area who did not know it. There had been many times in the past when she would end up racing one young buck or other who was out in his curricle. Sometimes she won and sometimes she did not. It did not matter a whit what the result of the contest was. Elizabeth enjoyed the race itself.

A few minutes later, as she reached the

edge of Meryton, she slowed down. She felt the flush of joy in her cheeks and was aware that her smile stretched from ear to ear. *Bless Papa,* she thought. *I needed that.*

~~~***~~~

That evening, Darcy entered Longbourn between Bingley and Madison and in front of the Hursts. He took a deep breath and braced himself. He knew that when he laid eyes on Elizabeth, everything else was going to cease to exist for him. He blew the breath out and twisted his neck to move the restricting cravat a little out of his way.

The group handed their outerwear to a maid and then greeted their host and hostess before moving on to the daughters of the house. As Darcy had expected, once he saw Elizabeth, he could think of no one and nothing else. It was only Madison's shove to his shoulder that got him moving again, a blush covering him from his neck to his hairline. He bowed to the younger girls and then followed Bingley into the drawing room, where a servant was busy passing out drinks. The three gentlemen found a quiet corner in which to observe the rest of the guests. They were soon joined by the Hursts.

Bingley had positioned himself so that he could see into the hallway. "Did Miss Bennet not look absolutely lovely?"

"All of them did." Louisa stood quietly beside her husband as she observed the guests filling the room. She smiled at those who greeted her.

"I confess I did not pay Miss Bennet much notice." Darcy sipped his port.

Madison snorted. "That is because you could not take your eyes off Miss Elizabeth." He laughed, as did Bingley and both of the Hursts.

Darcy felt himself grow hot all over. "All the Bennet women are beautiful in their own way." He glared at his friend. "I see you staring at the door as much as Bingley is. Waiting for someone specific, are you?" He nodded when Madison turned as red as he was.

"Now, gentlemen, no arguing." Hurst chuckled as he tucked his wife's hand under his elbow. "There are enough pretty girls here for everyone."

Darcy rolled his eyes as Bingley and Madison teased Hurst for his comments. He turned his attention back to the doorway, watching for the ladies to enter. As he waited, he reminded himself of all the reasons an attachment to Miss Elizabeth Bennet was probably not a good idea. He repeated over and over in his head the strikes she had against her: wildly inappropriate sisters, a loud and brash mother, little to no fortune, and no connections worth noting. His brain was fully convinced against her. It was his heart that objected. As usual, however, all his good intentions went out the window the moment he looked into her eyes.

"Miss Elizabeth." Darcy bowed to her, holding his breath as she curtseyed and then smiled at him when she rose.

"Mr. Darcy. How good of you to come. Do you enjoy cards?" Elizabeth's eyes twinkled as she lifted the corners of her lips into a small smile.

"I like them as much as any man, I suppose." Darcy could not resist the twitch of his lips in response to hers. "I am more skilled with some games than with others."

Elizabeth opened her mouth to reply, but before she could, her mother entered the room and called for everyone's attention.

In the end, Darcy was able to spend precious little time with Elizabeth. At first, he made up a fourth at whist at Mrs. Bennet's table, wondering at her cold treatment of him. Then, after that, he partnered with other people for other games. The night ended without him doing more than watching the object of his affections from the other side of the room for most of the night.

Chapter 5

Bingley, Darcy, Madison, and Hurst entered the rear dining room of the tavern, where the officers of the militia and many of the local landowners were gathered.

"Welcome, gentlemen." Colonel Forster, the officer in charge of the regiment, bowed. "Dinner should be served shortly." He pulled a watch out of a pocket and examined it. "I told the tavern keeper to have it served at six and it is just gone that now."

Bingley spoke for his friends. "Thank you for having us. We have been looking forward to becoming better acquainted with you all."

The colonel inclined his head. "I have, as well. Better relationships with the locals makes our time here much easier." He waved a hand in the direction of the long tables behind him. "You may sit wherever you wish."

With a murmur of thanks, Darcy and his friends walked further into the room. He nudged Bingley. "There are four empty seats right here, unless you prefer to be on the other side."

"Here is fine." Bingley looked at Hurst and Madison. "What do you think?"

Both men were agreeable and so the four

headed toward the chairs nearest to them. However, they were hailed by others and soon became separated. In the end, Darcy found himself sitting between Mr. Denny, who held the rank of captain, and a young man who had been introduced to him as Mr. Robert Lucas, son of Sir William Lucas. Across the table was a lieutenant named Saunderson, flanked by Bingley and Mr. Long.

Darcy was pleased with his dining companions. He had always found it easier to converse with other men, and even though he often found small talk tedious, he enjoyed the discussions to be had about everything from the war on the continent to the increased use of machines in manufacturing.

The first course had been served, eaten, and removed when a sudden change of conversational topic caught Darcy by surprise.

"Lucas! I saw Miss Elizabeth out in her father's gig this afternoon. I asked if she had beaten you recently. She blushed prettily and replied that you appeared to be too frightened to bring yours out and had therefore denied her the pleasure." Mr. Long leaned back, a twinkle in his eye, as he smirked at the young man to Darcy's left.

Lucas blushed deeply and cleared his throat. "Frightened, indeed." He lifted his chin. "I simply have too much sense to race a lady." He rolled his eyes when the rest of the local gentlemen roared with laughter.

A deep crease furrowed Bingley's brow. "What do you mean?"

Mr. Long leaned forward to see around the lieutenant. "Mr. Bennet has an old gig that he keeps in top condition. He taught his second daughter how to drive it. One or the other of them is nearly always out and about on it, and Miss Elizabeth loves to drive as fast as she can." He tipped his head toward Robert. "She has raced many of the young men of the area, and some of their fathers, as well. She nearly always wins. She is fearless behind a horse."

Darcy tried to suppress a grin. In his mind's eye, he could picture the lady in question, flushed and laughing in triumph.

Hurst had stopped eating to listen. "Does her father know she races?"

Mr. Long shrugged. "I should think so. She has made no secret of it, except possibly to her mother." He shuddered. "That woman can be rather vocal in her disapprobation."

Hurst raised his brow. "How interesting. Are any of these organized races?"

Robert Lucas shook his head. "Oh, no. Not usually. Most of the time, Miss Lizzy comes upon some unsuspecting gentleman in his equipage, stops beside him, and greets him charmingly. Before he knows it, he is careening down the road just beside her, urging his animals to run faster." He shrugged. "And suddenly, she is past him and all is lost."

The men around Darcy began to tease Lucas, but Darcy became lost in thought. *So, Miss Elizabeth races her father's carriage. I should very much like to see that.*

Later, as he and his friends travelled back to Netherfield, they began to discuss what they had learned.

"I can imagine Miss Elizabeth Bennet racing a gig, can you not, Darcy? She is a lively one."

"Yes, Bingley, I can," Darcy replied. "I would not mind having an opportunity to challenge her, to be honest. It is too bad my curricle is at Pemberley."

Madison chuckled. "Miss Lucas told me the last time I saw her that her friend was a good driver. I wondered at the time how she knew. I have never seen Miss Elizabeth doing anything other than walking."

"Nor I." Darcy paused. "She is unlike any other woman I have known."

"Her sister is, as well." Bingley sighed.

"I would venture to say the ladies in the country are far superior in many ways to those in town," Madison said. "They are, perhaps, not as wealthy and well-connected, and some lean towards being downright wild, but they have their charms."

None of them had a reply, so the rest of the short trip home was made in silence, each gentleman with his mind on one particular woman.

~~~***~~~

The next morning, Darcy was out early to exercise his horse when he heard the sound of a carriage on the nearby road. He stopped and turned, looking to see who was out in an equipage so early. To his surprise, it was Mr. Bennet and Elizabeth in what must be the gig he had been told about. The pair flew past so quickly that he was not certain they had seen him. However, they slowed and were soon trotting in his direction once again. He was unsurprised when they stopped nearby and beckoned to him.

"Good morning!" Mr. Bennet seemed to be in a cheerful frame of mind. "It is a beautiful day for a ride, is it not?"

"It is, indeed." Darcy tipped his hat to the gentleman and then to Miss Elizabeth. "What a beautiful gig you have there."

"Thank you. It was my father's. I keep it in good repair so I can continue to enjoy it." He nodded toward Elizabeth. "I have taught my daughter to drive it, as well. She enjoys walking a great deal, but every once in a while, I let her loose with it."

The corners of Darcy's lips tipped upwards. "Do you enjoy driving, Miss Bennet?"

Elizabeth smiled. "I confess I do, though I rarely keep to a sedate pace."

"No?" Darcy's brows rose. He did not want her to know he was aware of her penchant for racing but he was also surprised that she would even hint at having it.

"No. If I am going to be travelling on wheels, I prefer to make the trip as quickly as possible. After all, is that not the point of a carriage? To get one to their destination faster than walking will allow?" She arched a brow and batted her eyes at him.

Darcy strove to hide his amusement. "I suppose that is a logical assumption to make."

Elizabeth laughed and Mr. Bennet chuckled, shaking his head. "Logical, indeed." The mare suddenly shifted and his attention was momentarily focused on calming her. When she was still again, he looked back at Darcy.

"Elizabeth takes after me in many ways, and one of those is her fascination with carriages of all sorts." He glanced at his daughter before he continued. "I am endlessly proud of her. She is as daring as she is intelligent. I could not ask for a better child."

Darcy saw Elizabeth blush at her father's praise. He forced his attention away from the charming sight. "That is wonderful to hear. I have always believed that every child is worthy of being cherished, the girls as well as the boys. It is not right for young ladies to be uneducated and neglected simply because they are girls."

Bennet nodded. "Quite right. I will say, though, that if a particular girl chooses to remain ignorant even when given the opportunity to learn, then her fate is on her own head."

Darcy dipped his chin. "I had not considered such an event." He smiled. "I will grant you the right of being correct for the moment. However, I will contemplate this further and may change my mind later."

Bennet laughed, as did Elizabeth.

"Well," the older gentleman said, adjusting the reins in his hands. "We must be on our way. It was good to see you. I expect you and your friends will stop by and see us again soon. You will be most welcome." With a nod, Bennet slapped the reins and the carriage sprang into motion.

Darcy watched it as it drove away and noticed Elizabeth looking back for just a moment. He raised his hand and was rewarded with a return wave. Then, as quickly as they had appeared, the Bennets and their gig were gone. Darcy sat silently for a few minutes, remembering the encounter and analyzing the conversations. Finally, he turned his horse toward the stables and kicked it into motion.

Longbourn

October 29, 1811

Elizabeth was relaxing into a chair in the drawing room, her legs swinging off the arm of it, immersed in a book. Her sisters were spread out across the room similarly engaged, and her mother was lying on a sofa, a small plate of sugary confections resting on her chest. Mr. Bennet was in his book room, where he generally stayed during the day unless he was out attending to estate matters with his steward. The room was quiet for once. With the exception of an occasional giggle from the youngest girls, noise was nothing louder than a quiet hum. Suddenly, the rattle of an equipage coming toward the house shattered the peace of the afternoon.

Kitty jumped up at the sound to look out the window. "We have visitors, but I do not recognize the carriage."

Elizabeth and her mother sat up. Jane rose gracefully, setting her stitching on the table beside her. Mary looked up from the extracts she had been making, and Lydia joined her sister at the window.

"It is a gentleman." Kitty had her cheek pressed to the glass as she endeavored to see who had come. "I have never seen him before. Lydia, have you?"

Lydia mimicked her elder sister's actions but quickly drew back, her nose wrinkling. "No, I have not."

Just then, the ladies could hear knocking on the front door. They quickly put away their projects, or in Mrs. Bennet's case, their treats, and arranged themselves to properly greet the visitor.

"Mr. William Collins, ma'am." Mrs. Hill dipped a curtsey as the stranger, a tall, heavyset man in the clothing of a clergyman, entered the room.

"Welcome to Longbourn, sir." Mrs. Bennet

had narrowed her eyes at their guest, and Elizabeth wondered at it. "To what do we owe such a visit?"

Before Mr. Collins could reply, Mr. Bennet entered the room, the housekeeper right behind him. "Mr. Collins." He bowed to the clergyman. "This is quite unexpected. I had no idea you wished to visit our home."

Mr. Collins lifted his chin. "As you may have heard, my father recently passed on to his eternal reward. I thought it behooved me, once I learned of my inheritance, to visit and discover for myself what sort of place it was. In addition, I was recently and most generously granted a living in Kent from my most esteemed and benevolent patroness, Lady Catherine de Bourgh. It was she who urged me to introduce myself to you. I assure you that I come prepared to extend an olive branch to you and your family, the reason being that I, even before I rose in position to that of venerated rector, have never been comfortable with the anger and resentment my father held toward you, and I feel that it is incumbent upon me as a spiritual leader and example to all those in my sphere to heal the breach if I can. The Scriptures are clear that, as far as it depends upon me, I am to live at peace with everyone." He paused, but only long enough to take a breath. "You cannot be averse to a visit from such a personage as I am, given that I am to inherit and those doing the work of the Lord are to be welcomed into the homes of

61

everyone and fed and clothed as needed." He gestured toward the ladies. "I had heard that your daughters were comely creatures and I see that they are. What a blessing they must be to you. I detest the thought of injuring them; hence my offer of an olive branch, an offer that you cannot be inclined to deny."

Chapter 6

Mr. Collins paused to take another breath and Elizabeth, eyes wide and brow wrinkled, turned her gaze to her father to see how he planned to handle the situation.

Mr. Bennet had begun smirking as Collins' long-winded speech wore on. Now, however, he seemed to want to put a stop to any further monologues. "It is considered quite rude for someone, even a rector such as yourself, to spring themselves unannounced upon a household. Are you expecting to stay here, or have you let a room at the inn?"

"Why, here, of course. You cannot expect someone in as exalted a position as I am in to sleep at an inn, surely?"

Elizabeth rolled her eyes. The man was ridiculous.

"Mr. Bennet-" Her mother started to say something, but stopped.

Mr. Bennet glanced quickly at his wife but immediately returned his focus to the newcomer. "I can expect just that, in light of the fact that you have given us no warning of your arrival. However, it would be ungentlemanly of me to do so, and no matter how poor your manners are, I will not forgo my upbringing just to make a point." Longbourn's master gestured toward his wife and daughters. "Allow me to introduce you to my family."

Collins had stiffened during his exchange

with Mr. Bennet, but now turned toward the ladies with what Elizabeth could only describe as an ingratiating smile. "Of course."

"In the middle is my wife, who clearly recognized your name, though she has never laid eyes on you before. To her right is my eldest daughter, Jane. On Mrs. Bennet's other side is my second daughter, Elizabeth. Standing in front of the table is my middle child, Mary, and by the window are my youngest girls, Catherine and Lydia. Mrs. Bennet, girls, this is Mr. Collins, who, it seems, will inherit Longbourn when I am gone."

Each of the ladies had curtseyed when introduced. Strangely, even the youngest remained silent. Finally, Mr. Bennet cleared his throat. His wife flattened her lips but invited the rector to sit.

Choosing a chair next to the one Elizabeth had recently occupied, Mr. Collins began a new monologue, showering praise upon every aspect of the estate that he had seen so far, including the furnishings in the present room. He sat, without waiting for the ladies to be seated first, and Elizabeth looked at her father with her brow raised and her eyes twinkling. *Oh,* she thought, *this ought to be fun.* She settled down on the sofa beside her mother and tried not to grin when Mr. Bennet winked. She turned her attention back to their guest.

"Now that I think upon it, I realize that you must be alarmed at my coming so precipitously. I assure you, I intend no harm. I simply come to admire. Might I say again, Mrs. Bennet, that your daughters have lived up to their reputations as beauties. I am happy to learn that the rumors I heard are true. So often these things are exaggerated, but in your case, that is not so. You have every reason to be proud of their loveliness."

Mrs. Bennet's countenance instantly changed. She had never been one to discount any praise heaped upon her girls and now, even though she clearly distrusted their visitor, she preened under his admiration for them. "Thank you, sir. I hope to marry them off soon. Things are settled here so strangely that I know not how I will maintain them if Mr. Bennet were to pass away."

"You refer to the entail, of course. My patroness, the Right Honorable Lady Catherine de Bourgh, recently told me that her late husband's family was opposed to the idea of entailing an estate away from the females of the family, and so her daughter, Miss Anne de Bourgh, the premier jewel of Kent, is named as the heir of Rosings, the beautiful estate they live on. Of course, my ancestors did not share this view, which means I will inherit on the unhappy day when your husband meets his Maker." Collins paused long enough to make a sad face. "But hopefully that day is far away and you may enjoy this beautiful home for many more years."

Mr. Bennet cleared his throat, drawing the attention of his heir presumptive as well as his wife and children. "You mentioned that your father has left this mortal coil. I had not heard of it. I cannot say I regret him, given our history; however, allow me to extend my condolences for your loss. I remember when my father passed on. It was a difficult time. I would not wish that experience on anyone." He paused, but before Collins could reply, spoke again. "What possessed you to so impulsively decide to attend us here?"

Collins' eyes widened. "Oh, I did not explain myself, did I? Allow me to apologize. You see, my most esteemed patroness, Lady Catherine, instructed me to come. She insisted that it was imperative that I learn more of the estate and its occupants. She suggested the extension of an olive branch as a way to heal the breach between our families and ease the burden you all must assuredly carry." He paused and took a breath. Mr. Bennet interrupted him.

"Indeed. Well, as I said before, you are welcome to remain, since you are now here." Bennet's brow creased and his mien was somber as he continued. "If there are to be any future visits, I will insist upon being warned ahead of time. Lady Catherine de Bourgh may not mind unwanted visitors, but I do. If you arrive a second time without seeking my permission first, you will be turned away with no remorse on my part."

Mr. Collins looked alarmed. Elizabeth had to turn her head into her shoulder to muffle the giggles that bubbled up at his widened eyes and fluttering hands. She dared not look at her father or any of her sisters lest she burst out into wild guffaws and offend their visitor or her parents.

"Of course! Absolutely! I will not fail to write to you first."

Bennet made a gesture with his hand and immediately, the rector clamped his lips shut.

"Mrs. Bennet, girls, this gentleman is, as you may have already deduced, the son of my third cousin twice removed, Mr. Harcourt Collins. You have never met this man or his father or any other of his family because, as our guest has indicated, there was a disagreement between them and my own family. I will not ask you to treat this stranger as if he were one of your other cousins, but I do expect you to behave toward him as you would any other guest. Do you have any questions?" Bennet looked at his wife and each of his daughters in turn. None of them replied, so he clapped his hands on the arm of his chair and stood. "Very well, then. I will retire to my book room until supper. Mr. Collins, I believe my housekeeper has a room in the guest wing being prepared for you. I will instruct her to escort you to it when it is ready." He bowed. "Wife, I await your summons for supper."

Collins and the ladies had risen when the

master of the house had and now made their own bows and curtseys. Once the door had closed behind Mr. Bennet, they sank back down into seats. There was silence for a few brief moments, but then Mr. Collins began speaking and after that, there was no opportunity for anyone else to.

Later, after Mrs. Hill had removed their guest from the room, the ladies all collapsed into their chairs and breathed a collective sigh.

"La, he can talk! I thought he was never going to stop!" Lydia's head lolled to the side, making it easier for her to see her mother.

Elizabeth laughed. "It is a wonder he did not wear himself out, is it not?"

Kitty reached for the paper and pencil she kept at hand for sketching. "Maybe he will be so tired from it that he will not open his lips at supper."

"Girls! You must not speak so of him." Mrs. Bennet paused and tilted her head. "Though, I must say I hope the same."

Jane's eyes grew wide. "Mama!"

"Oh, hush, Jane." Mrs. Bennet lifted her chin. "You feel the same, I am certain."

"I wonder what he meant by 'an olive branch'?" Mary had followed her younger sister's example and brought her book of sermons and her paper and pencil back out.

Mrs. Bennet shook her head. "I do not know. I cannot imagine what he could possibly do that might ease our discomfort with the
68

entail and the prospect of being thrown into the hedgerows."

Elizabeth and her sisters all murmured their agreement and sat quietly for a while. Elizabeth spent the time pondering her cousin and his olive branch. She assumed the other girls were doing the same, as silent as they were. Eventually, Mrs. Bennet rose, reminding them of the time, and they separated, each to her own chamber, to prepare for dinner.

The evening meal came and went, and soon the family found themselves trapped in the drawing room with Mr. Collins and his unstoppable conversation. *Well,* Elizabeth thought, *it is not actual conversation, is it, since he rarely allows anyone else to participate.* The act of pretending to listen was wearing on her and, based on their yawns and rolling eyes, her sisters. Finally, Mr. Bennet rose and said good night, escorting his wife and daughters out of the room. Collins followed, chattering all the way.

~~~***~~~

The following evening, Mrs. Bennet discovered just what her guest was about, and it delighted her.

Collins had spent the entire day with Elizabeth and her sisters, giving the most attention to Jane. One or the other of the girls was forever rescuing her from his clutches, because Jane was incapable of being rude or even seeing the bad in others. Eventually, the rector gave up the pursuit and followed his cousin into his book room for the rest of the afternoon. His behavior continued through dinner that evening, and it was afterwards, when the family was gathered in the drawing room, that he pulled his hostess aside.

"You are aware, I hope, that I have recently been granted a generous living by my most condescending and esteemed patroness, Lady Catherine de Bourgh."

Mrs. Bennet nodded stiffly. "Indeed, I am aware." She was not going to make it easy for this leech to convey anything to her.

"She has shared her wise counsel with me and suggested that I come to Longbourn to find a wife from among your daughters. They are all quite beautiful, though Miss Bennet far outshines the rest, given that she is the image of you and you are a very attractive woman. I have given it much consideration and I believe that she would do very nicely as the companion of my future life."

Mrs. Bennet had inwardly rejoiced once she heard the word "wife." However, when he indicated Jane as his choice, she paused in her silent exaltations. She bit her lip as she thought. Mr. Collins would inherit her house when her husband passed, and that was attractive, but Mr. Bingley had indicated interest and he had five thousand pounds a year. She glanced at Jane, her twin in beauty and grace, and made her decision. "I am afraid, sir, that there is one who has come before you for Jane. However, none of the other girls are attached in any way."

Collins' face fell. "I see." He turned to examine the other girls more carefully. He heard squeals of laughter from the youngest two and ruled them out as too young and immature. Mary was accomplished and seemed the most serious. She might do, but for the fact that she was the plainest of them. He then looked at Elizabeth. She was every bit as lovely as Jane and was far more serious than her youngest sisters, though apparently not as studious as Mary. She was graceful and elegant, though. She smiled too much and laughed too freely, but he was certain she would make an excellent wife and would be so in awe of his patroness as to never giggle or smile in her presence. He turned to Mrs. Bennet.

"Miss Elizabeth?"

The matron nodded. "I know of no others who have expressed interest in her. You may have her."

Collins grinned, rubbing his hands together. "Thank you, madam."

Mrs. Bennet shooed him away. "Think nothing of it. Go and charm her, then."

Collins moved away, parking himself as near to Elizabeth as he could get and refusing to budge.

That night, as Elizabeth was preparing for

bed, she thought about the strange way in which her father's cousin had transferred his attention from her elder sister to her. She could not determine a reason for it, though she had seen the man in conference with her mother early in the evening. Mrs. Bennet had seemed happy afterwards, so whatever they had spoken about had pleased her. She shrugged. It was a mystery and not one she was going to solve at the moment. She crawled into bed, her mind on a different gentleman entirely.

~~~***~~~

For the next two or three days, Mr. Collins remained as close to Elizabeth as possible. She wondered a time or two what he was up to and if he had chosen marriage to her as his olive branch to the family. However, she saw no point in borrowing trouble and so endeavored to ignore that possibility, and her cousin, as much and as often as she could.

Chapter 7

Darcy, Madison, and the Bingley party had been among the first to arrive at Lucas Lodge. This had been the result of two things: Madison was eager to spend time with Charlotte Lucas, and Bingley was keen to speak to Jane Bennet. Though he would not admit to it, Darcy felt the same about Elizabeth. He was still uncertain about how to proceed, though he admitted to himself that he was, at the least, infatuated with her. He knew it was unlike him to be so indecisive. He could not help himself, though, and he was aware that all rational thought flew out of his head when in her presence, even if they never spoke. If they were in the same room, he was befuddled. That was all there was to it. As a result, he was both nervous about seeing her and looking forward to it. He shifted to his other foot as he watched the doorway.

Bingley nudged him. "Will you please stand still? All this fidgeting about is unsettling."

Darcy spun his head toward his friend. "I apologize. I did not realize I was doing it. I will endeavor to stop." He glanced around. "What happened to Madison?"

Bingley nodded toward the side of the room.

"He has found Miss Lucas and has abandoned us for her."

Darcy looked in the direction indicated, soon locating his friend and the lady in question. "Is he serious about her, do you think?"

"Oh, I would say so." Bingley looked at Darcy with a cocked brow. "Have you ever seen him so taken with a woman before? You know as well as I do that he is too upright to trifle with one." He gestured toward the man in question. "Do you see how he blushes? She does, as well. I would not be at all surprised if there is an engagement announced very soon."

Darcy tilted his head as he watched Madison smile at Charlotte. "I confess I have not seen him so enamored of a lady before. I hope that if a match is made, they are very happy together. He deserves it, and from what I understand, so does Miss Lucas."

Bingley's reply was drowned out by the sound of new voices. Darcy looked toward the room's doorway and saw Mr. and Mrs. Bennet enter. He nudged his friend. When Elizabeth followed behind them, his heart suddenly thumped hard in his chest and he let out a breath he had not realized he was holding.

"Excuse me, Darcy. I am certain I will see you in a few minutes." Bingley did not wait for a reply, walking instantly away and in Jane's direction.

Darcy would have liked to follow. Elizabeth was at her sister's side, after all. He looked down and chewed his lip for a second, willing his heart to stop racing. Instead of giving in to his urge to speak to her, he forced himself to remain stationary.

Soon, the meal was announced. Darcy, as the highest ranking male in attendance, escorted his hostess into the dining room. Sir William followed with Mrs. Hurst, and the others trailed behind according to precedence.

When Darcy had seated Lady Lucas and taken his own place, his attention was caught by the constant chatter of a gentleman he had never met before who sat across the table and down a bit. His brow creased when he thought he heard his aunt's name, but though he was close enough to hear the man's voice, he could not make out everything that was said. He shrugged to himself and looked for Elizabeth. Unfortunately, she was on the same side of the table as he was, so he could not see her. With a quiet sigh, he turned his attention to the food on his plate and his dinner companions.

Once the meal was completed and the ladies had retired to the drawing room, Darcy began to feel more comfortable. He accepted a glass of port from his host and chatted with the gentlemen nearest to him. He was deep into a discussion about the revolts in manufacturing in the north when he was suddenly addressed by the man who had been so talkative earlier.

"Mr. Darcy."

Darcy looked away from his conversational partner with his brow creased, to give his attention to the other man, who bowed deeply.

"I know it is not the normal course of things, but I fancy that, given my exalted and respected position as a clergyman, it will not be looked at askance for me to introduce myself to you. I am William Collins. I have recently been granted the rectory at Hunsford by your liberal and honored aunt, Lady Catherine de Bourgh, who, when I saw her last just three days ago, was in perfect health, as was her daughter, Miss de Bourgh."

Darcy flicked his eyes up and down the strange man's person before he replied. "I thank you for the information. I received a letter from her this past Tuesday assuring me of her condition and that of her household. I am happy to know that she did not suddenly fall ill after sending it."

"I could do nothing else. Her condescension to one of my humble but revered position is matchless in society, I daresay. She has given me much excellent advice and seen to the care of my abode as though it were her own. Why, just last week, she inspected my closets and ordered shelves installed in two of them. She has spoken to my housekeeper, as well, on the proper methods of cleaning. I am honored to be under her gracious care."

Darcy could only stare as the other gentleman carried on in the same vein for several more minutes. *He seems to both believe he is above my aunt and below her,* he thought. *And who in their right mind would enjoy Aunt Catherine ordering his life for him?* He was about to tell the man to leave off when Sir William rose and suggested they all join the ladies.

In the drawing room, Darcy immediately searched for Elizabeth, finding her near the pianoforte with Charlotte Lucas. He followed behind Bingley and Madison, who clearly had located their ladies and were headed in that direction.

"At last you are here." Elizabeth smiled at the gentlemen. "I had feared Sir William would keep you all in the dining room until it was time to leave." Her eyes sparkled in amusement when her friend and Jane, who was standing with them, giggled behind their fans.

"Tease them all you like, Eliza," Charlotte said. "You know what comes next. We must have music and we have volunteered to play first."

Elizabeth sighed dramatically and rolled her eyes. "Indeed, I do. You will have me torture these lovely gentlemen with my poor playing. I am certain they have heard much better than me."

"Ah, Miss Elizabeth," Bingley replied. "Miss Bennet assures me that you are a fine player who charms her listeners." He nudged Darcy. "We are eager to hear you."

Elizabeth pursed her lips as though trying to hide a smile. "Very well, then. You cannot say you were not warned." She turned to her friend. "Charlotte has agreed to turn the pages for me and I for her." With that, she stepped behind the instrument, Charlotte right behind her, and sat down on the bench, lifting her fingers and placing them on the keys.

Darcy found that Elizabeth's playing was everything lovely. While not technically perfect, she played with feeling, and that elevated her performance to exactly what Jane had said it would be: charming. He found himself entranced with the music and with watching her as she moved back and forth following the movement of her hands up and down the keyboard. He was so involved with it that he jumped when Bingley nudged him and leaned closer.

"Miss Bennet was correct. Miss Elizabeth plays very well."

Darcy nodded at his friend's quiet words, unable to remove his eyes from Elizabeth, even to whisper a reply. "Indeed."

All too soon for Darcy's liking, the song was over. He continued to stare as Elizabeth turned the pages for her friend. Then, when Charlotte's exhibition was completed, Mary Bennet took over the instrument. Mary had none of her sister's feeling, though she was technically proficient. Her performance was not nearly as pleasing and though he had determined to remain in his seat and not seek Elizabeth out, he was unable to maintain the pleasant focus he had previously enjoyed. He stood from his chair and approached the table where tea was being served, accepting a cup from the servant there and taking a sip as he took up a place near the door. He proceeded to sip his tea and watch the rest of the party, doing his best to keep his eyes off the lady he most longed to speak to. When his tea was finished, he took the empty cup back to the table and gave it to the maid, then wandered toward the other side of the room.

A rush of younger ladies, two of whom Darcy knew as Elizabeth's youngest sisters, surrounded the pianoforte, and he heard them demand music for dancing.

"That is a wonderful idea!" Sir William, who had joined the girls gathered around the instrument, clapped his hands. "I know you do not favor such tunes, Miss Mary, but surely you cannot deny us the pleasure."

Darcy heard the middle Bennet daughter agree to play and watched as Sir William beamed at her before urging the young men to clear the middle of the floor.

The first set of dances was complete in short order. Darcy had found a spot near the fireplace to watch the proceedings. As another young lady – Darcy was uncertain who she was, though he was positive they had been introduced – took over at the pianoforte, his ear was caught by the voice of Mrs. Bennet. He heard her second daughter's name and, though it was beneath him to eavesdrop, shamelessly listened in.

"Mr. Collins has a very good living, you know. He will marry Lizzy and the family will be saved from the hedgerows when Mr. Bennet dies."

Darcy's breath caught.

"Has he proposed already? Will she have him?"

His eyes closed as he waited the Bennet matriarch's reply.

"She will marry him or I will never speak to her again. I cannot maintain her when her father is gone, and it is her duty to marry and marry well."

"I cannot see her father forcing her if she refuses."

"I have my ways of getting what I wish. Trust me, Lizzy will marry Mr. Collins. She is not likely to receive any other offers and she will be easily worked on to do her duty."

Darcy heard nothing else. His eyes popped open as his entire body clenched. *No*, he thought. *It cannot be true. My beautiful, lively Elizabeth with that ridiculous toad of a man?*

The longer he thought about her being married to anyone but him, the larger the ache in his chest grew. He began to panic. *I must stop this travesty. She is mine and I love her. I will not give her up!* His head began to turn this way and that as he searched her out. Finally locating her across the room and next to the open area in the middle where the dancers were lining up for another set, he strode toward her. He saw her look at him and smile as he approached.

Darcy grabbed Elizabeth's hand and pulled her into his arms. He looked deep into her eyes and saw the emotions flashing through them: surprise, at first, followed quickly by warmth and a welcome. He glanced down at her lips to see they were parted slightly, and back up. His heart pounded when he saw her own dark eyes drift down his face and stop just above his chin. He swallowed and slowly, ever so slowly, he lowered his face toward her, rejoicing inside when she lifted hers to meet his kiss. He brushed her mouth with his and then did it again before settling over her lips. He clutched her to him, binding her tightly to his chest with his arms. He was insensible to anything but the scent of lavender in her hair and the sensation of her body pressed tightly to his. She moaned and he answered. Only a need for air brought the moment to a close. He pressed his forehead against hers as they gasped in unison.

"Elizabeth," he whispered. He became aware of her arms around his waist and smiled. He kissed her forehead before resting his cheek in her hair.

As his breathing returned to normal, he heard screams from the other side of the room. Suddenly, a voice, harsh and angry, came from beside him.

"Unhand my daughter, sir!"

Darcy jumped, as did Elizabeth. They separated, reluctantly on his part, and he watched her blush. He realized as he noticed the stares and the silence that he had caused a scene.

Mr. Bennet glowered at them. "A word, if you please." He turned to Sir William, who had appeared at his side. "May we use your study?"

"Of course! You know the way?"

"I do." Mr. Bennet turned to the couple. "Elizabeth, Mr. Darcy." He pointed toward the doorway that led to the hall.

A minute later and the three of them were standing in the middle of the small room their host claimed as his. Mr. Bennet cleared his throat. "Normally, I would laugh at folly such as what you and Lizzy have done and send you on your way with a strongly worded reprimand and that would be that. However, after that kiss, I am afraid that I must insist that you marry her."

Darcy smiled. "I would be honored to." He turned to Elizabeth as her father harrumphed.

"Elizabeth?" Mr. Bennet's tone indicated his disappointment in her behavior.

Though Darcy thought he should probably feel guilty about leading Elizabeth into such improper conduct, he found he could not. He watched as she kept her eyes focused on his even as she replied to her father.

"I would be happy to marry Mr. Darcy." She smiled.

Mr. Bennet did not reply for a moment. When he did, all he said was, "Well, then." He cleared his throat. "Are you quite certain?"

"I am, Papa. I have longed for Mr. Darcy's attention for weeks. I love him."

The older gentleman's lips turned down at the corners. He sighed. "Very well. It was necessary anyway but if you were made unhappy, I would have found a way to prevent it." He turned to Darcy. "I do not at all approve of your method of gaining a wife, young man. I am angry that you chose to compromise my daughter in front of all the neighbors instead of courting her properly." His shoulders slumped. "However, the deed is done and there is no help for it." He straightened and looked Darcy in the eye. "If you harm my Lizzy in any way, you will answer to me. Do I make myself clear?"

Darcy nodded. "Yes, sir. I promise you, I will cherish her for the rest of her days. She will never want for anything. I love her and cannot live without her."

Bennet's lips pressed together for a moment. "I am glad to hear it," he finally said. "Come; let us go announce the engagement."

Darcy and Elizabeth followed her father back into the drawing room, where Mr. Bennet announced the betrothal to the neighbors.

"It seems as though my Lizzy and Mr. Darcy are to be married. Congratulations to the happy couple."

At first, the silence remained, but then suddenly became a cacophony of noise. Elizabeth's sisters and friends surrounded her, congratulating her on her engagement and exclaiming over the romantic and dramatic nature of the betrothal. Darcy could hear other voices whispering about the event in a much more disapproving tone of voice. He shrugged to himself. He had his heart's desire, and had saved his love from a life tied to a ridiculous man who kowtowed to his demanding aunt. That was all that mattered.

Chapter 8

"No! I will not have it!" Mrs. Bennet's shrill voice suddenly rose above all the others. "She is to marry Mr. Collins and *only* Mr. Collins! You must stop this travesty, Mr. Bennet!"

Darcy, Elizabeth, and everyone else in the room stopped speaking and looked toward the mistress of Longbourn.

Mr. Bennet scowled and, with a roll of his eyes, moved from his daughter's side to his wife's. He took her elbow. "Come, Mrs. Bennet. We will discuss this in private." Though his wife tried to dig her heels in, refusing to be silent, he urged her forward, not allowing her reluctance to persuade him to stop. Her voice, which had never ceased protesting both Elizabeth's engagement to Darcy and her husband's manhandling of her person, soon faded as he propelled her down the hall.

"Mrs. Bennet is correct. You have been promised to me, Miss Elizabeth, and are not free to marry anyone else. I am outraged at the unbecoming and wanton behavior I have just witnessed." Mr. Collins took hold of Elizabeth's free arm and tried to tug her away.

Elizabeth attempted to yank her limb out of her cousin's grasp. "This is not the place for such a discussion, sir," she hissed at him. "You never asked for my hand, and if you had, I would not grant it to you."

Darcy stepped between his betrothed and Mr.

Collins. "Let go of my future wife." He caught the other man's eye. "Or there will be consequences for you that will be life-altering." He paused. "I am Lady Catherine's favorite nephew and I have a great deal of influence on her." He winced inwardly, knowing that once his aunt found out about his engagement, he would likely fall in her esteem and his threat might be baseless. Outwardly, he maintained his cold look of hauteur.

Collins paused; fear appeared in his eyes. He let go of Elizabeth and stepped back. "As I understand it, once a living is granted, it cannot be taken away, especially from someone with my valued qualifications. However, your aunt, though a liberal mistress and generous beyond comprehension, could make my life difficult if she were so inclined. Therefore, I will leave off for now." He puffed himself up and pulled his waistcoat down. "I am not finished, though. I will see Miss Elizabeth betrothed to me before this night is over." He turned and exited the room.

Elizabeth, a blush spread over her entire countenance, turned to Darcy. "I am so sorry for my mother and my cousin. They are ..." She trailed off, clearly unable to find words to describe their behavior.

Darcy laid his free hand over hers, which rested in the crook of his elbow. "Fear not. I am not upset, at least not with you. I am surprised at your mother's reaction, I confess, but I would imagine Mr. Collins' disappointment at missing out on such a lovely bride is understandable."

A faint smile lifted Elizabeth's lips for just a moment, but then she became serious. Her eyes searched his. Finally, apparently seeing that he was telling the truth, she closed her eyes and sighed. She looked at him again and smiled fully. "Thank you for the compliment. I am sure it is untrue, but you seem to believe it, so I will not disabuse you of the notion." A glimmer of her usual good humor appeared when she smirked at him.

Darcy lifted her hand and pressed a kiss to the back. He remained close by her side the rest of the evening.

~~~***~~~

The next day, Darcy presented himself at Longbourn's door precisely at the time Mr. Bennet had ordered him to the day before. The housekeeper escorted him to a spacious room lined with bookshelves. Bennet rose from behind a desk near the single set of windows the space contained. Darcy bowed.

"Right on time, I see." Bennet gestured toward a pair of wingback chairs next to the fireplace located close to the desk. "Have a seat."

Darcy did as instructed, waiting for Bennet to follow him before he sat. "I want you to know that I was being truthful when I told you last evening that I love your daughter. I have admired her from a distance for weeks." He looked down. "I apologize for my behavior. I did not set out to compromise her. I have never behaved so with anyone before." He paused, lifting his hands in a gesture meant to indicate his uncertainty. "I heard your wife telling someone that she was promised to your heir and I fear I panicked."

Bennet snorted. "You feared not getting what you wished, so you rushed across the room and kissed Elizabeth like she was the last fresh water in the driest desert."

Darcy turned red. He tried to push down the affront he felt at Bennet's tone of voice. "Again, I apologize."

Bennet shook his head. "Do not take offense. I spoke at length with my daughter last night and have come to understand her feelings in the matter. She is not at all distressed about the whole thing, and so neither will I be." He paused. "Let me call for tea and we can discuss the settlement. My brother Phillips should be along shortly. He is the solicitor in Meryton and my representative. He will write up the initial agreement and have his clerk make copies." He rose and pulled the cord hanging beside the fireplace, then walked to the door. Darcy heard him ask for tea and instruct the servant to bring Mr. Phillips in as soon as he arrived.

Bennet returned to his chair, settling himself down into it once more. "I will have Lizzy called for once we have the basic elements of the marriage articles worked out. She is the most intelligent of my children and I wish for her to know what to expect in the future."

Darcy nodded. "I think that is an excellent plan." He hesitated. "Miss Elizabeth is your favorite?"

Bennet dipped his chin. "I probably should not have one, but I do and I confess she is it. Lizzy is just like me in every way, except that of sex." He looked at Darcy with a tiny crease in his brow. "I taught my daughter everything she knows of driving and horses and carriages, including their maintenance and construction. She gains a great deal of enjoyment from caring for my gig. My will names her as the one who will inherit it when I am gone." He gestured toward the door, beyond which Mrs. Bennet's strident voice could be heard berating someone. "None of the rest care for it at all, and my wife is horrified at the thought that one of her girls would be involved in activities that are not only unladylike but also menial." He shrugged. "I ignore her and have taught Lizzy to, as well. I warn you, however, that to deny her that outlet may not be a good idea."

"I have no intention of denying it to her. I am rather fond of my own curricle, so I understand the enjoyment she gets out of it." He paused, smiling down at his hands. "I confess I would love to race her. I have heard of the way she charmingly suggests it and then rejoices when she wins."

Bennet laughed. "And she wins quite often." He called out for the servant who had knocked on the door to enter and then said nothing else until the tea was served and the maid departed. "I am happy to hear that you will not restrict her in this." He took a sip out of his cup as he looked over the top of it. "She is very well-read and loves to debate."

Darcy lowered his teacup. "Sir, one of the things I love about your daughter is her intelligence. I have no desire for a stupid wife. I want someone to challenge me. I will not restrict her in anything except that which might endanger her beyond endurance. I will insist she does not drive about alone, or even walk by herself, especially when we are in town, and I will insist she keep me informed about her movements, but that is all. She only needs to tell someone ... the housekeeper or butler, my sister, or myself ... where she is going. I am not a gentleman who requires a wife to bend to his will in every aspect."

Bennet nodded. "Good, good. You should be very happy, then. I only wished to warn you that if you tried, she would make your life miserable." He winked.

Darcy laughed, an image forming in his mind of his betrothed with her hands on her hips, berating him.

Just then, the housekeeper announced Mr. Phillips and the gentlemen got down to the business of the marriage papers.

As the late morning hours turned into late afternoon, Darcy and Elizabeth left her father's library to take a stroll around the gardens. Jane and Bingley trailed behind them.

"Thank you for not objecting to my father's wish to include me in the discussion." Elizabeth looked up at her betrothed and smiled.

"It was nothing, I assure you." Darcy laid his free hand over hers where it rested on his arm and caressed her fingers. "I would not want you to worry about the future and what will happen should the unthinkable occur. Besides, what better way to assure myself that you will not be taken in by an unscrupulous relative when I am gone?" He stopped and turned toward her. "You are an intelligent woman, Elizabeth. I respect that." He paused and lifted his hand to cup her cheek. "It is one of the things that made me fall in love with you." He leaned down and brushed her lips with his.

Elizabeth grinned. "You may live to regret my intelligence when I question your every decision." She winked.

Darcy laughed, his eyes crinkling at the sides. "Never. It is not possible."

"Well, we shall see. Perhaps I will be obstinate on purpose just to try you."

Darcy pulled her closer just as the cold wind blew sharply around them. "I look forward to it." He glanced back down the path and, not seeing Bingley and Jane, who had agreed to chaperone, turned his attention back to the woman in his arms, who shivered as she looked at him with wide eyes. "You are cold," he whispered. "Let me warm you." He leaned down again and captured her lips. As had happened the night before, he lost himself in the feel of her. The snap of a twig brought him back to awareness, and he slowly ended the kiss. He whispered words of love in her ear before taking a step back.

From a few feet away, Jane called out to them. "Lizzy, Mary has been sent out to bring us in for dinner."

Elizabeth cleared her throat and looked down for a moment before lifting her eyes back to Darcy's. "We are coming, Jane." She addressed her betrothed. "Well, sir; shall we eat?"

Entranced by Elizabeth's blush and her sparkling eyes, Darcy only nodded. He turned them back toward Bingley and Jane and escorted her down the path and into the house.

After giving their outerwear to the housekeeper, the pair entered the drawing room. Immediately, Mr. Collins began a long speech on the proper behavior of young ladies. Mr. Bennet arrived shortly thereafter, and Collins ceased speaking entirely, his whole being exuding affront.

Darcy leaned toward Elizabeth, who was seated beside him on a sofa. "What has happened?"

Elizabeth looked at him and rolled her eyes. Her soft reply made Darcy's eyes widen. "He spent most of the day following me around, lecturing me on the same subject he just now did and declaring how he was certain he would soon make my father see reason and end my engagement to you. Mama had spent the morning doing something similar. Mr. Collins joined his arguments to hers until Papa called her into his book room not long before you arrived and apparently told her to leave off. She retired to her room but he has not left me alone since."

Darcy's brow creased. "Had you been aware that he wanted to marry you?"

She shrugged. "I wondered about it. He refused to be parted from me for two whole days and my mother was always pushing us together. However, my father would not have allowed it unless I truly wished it, and I did not."

Darcy's frown remained, but he took her hand and lifted it to his lips. "I am happy to hear it. I confess it was your mother who, without meaning to, pushed me to act as I did last night." He glanced at Collins, who was standing a few feet away and glaring at them. "I overheard her telling someone that she would force the match and ..." he paused, looking down and turning a deep red. "I was frantic that it not happen. I did not wish to lose you. I acted without thought. I should apologize, but ..." He looked up. "I am not the least bit sorry."

Elizabeth's lips lifted in a soft smile. "I am not sorry, either. Do not be distressed. I am incandescently happy to be engaged to you." She glanced around before leaning a bit closer to him so she could whisper her next words. "I thought it quite the romantic thing."

Darcy's eyes lit up. "I am pleased to hear it." He lifted her hand to bestow another kiss upon it when the sound of Collins' voice made him stop.

"I cannot believe, Miss Elizabeth, that your father sits right here in front of you and yet you throw yourself at Mr. Darcy. I can promise you that when we are wed, you will be soundly corrected for such wanton behavior." He took a breath and opened his mouth to continue when he was suddenly stopped by Mr. Bennet.

"That is enough, Mr. Collins." Bennet practically leaped out of his chair. "I told you that you will never marry my daughter and I meant it. As a matter of fact ..." He paused as he looked around at the rest of his offspring and their guests. "You will not marry *any* of my daughters. Not now and not ever. If any of them choose to accept you, I will disown them and they will not receive a penny after I am gone." He looked at each girl in turn, asking if they understood. When he received acknowledgement from them all, he turned back to his cousin. "If I hear one more word from you about it, I will demand that you leave and never return."

"Now see here! I am to inherit. I have every right to be in residence in this house."

"When I am dead you do. Not before. Until the moment I cock up my toes, this house remains mine and the only visitors that will come here will be those I invite. Do I make myself clear?"

Collins stood silently clutching his lapels and clenching his jaw. Finally, he bowed shallowly and replied. "Crystal clear." He turned and stomped to the corner of the room, where he slumped down into a chair and looked for all the world like a pouting child.

Darcy shook his head at the spectacle the clergyman made. He could not imagine behaving in such a manner. He looked at Elizabeth and his heart soared. "I am my beloved and my beloved is mine," he whispered before he lifted the hand he still held and kissed the back of it.

Mrs. Hill called them in to dinner at that moment and Darcy proudly escorted his betrothed into the dining room, sitting beside her and thereby displacing Mary.

"I apologize, Miss Mary." He stood and bowed. "May I help you with your chair?"

Mary turned red and looked down. "There is no need to apologize, sir. You are to be my brother; it is only right that you sit beside Lizzy."

"You are too kind." Darcy helped Mary sit, thinking as he did that she reminded him of a less-polished version of his own sister, Georgiana. He made a mental note to try to draw her out more often. However, as he settled into his own chair, it was Elizabeth who drew his attention, as it always did.

Chapter 9

Outside Mr. Phillips' office, Meryton

November 4, 1811

Elizabeth and her sisters walked into town to visit their aunt, Mrs. Phillips, in her apartment above her husband's office. Lydia and Kitty were in the front of the group, followed by Mary. Elizabeth and Jane walked close behind her, and bringing up the rear was Mr. Collins, who spent the entire quarter hour grumbling under his breath. The ladies were silent, except for the two youngest, who chattered all the way to their destination about the officers and how they hoped Denny had returned from London.

Mr. Phillips' office was located halfway up the high street of the village, across from the milliner and between the tobacco shop and the book shop. The Bennets and their cousin were two doors away when Lydia burst out in excitement.

"There he is! Denny!" She waved excitedly, squealing when he heard her and lifted his hand in greeting. "Come, Kitty, we must go greet him!"

As her two youngest sisters sped toward the gentleman at a near-run, Elizabeth shook her head. "I suppose there is no use in chastising them."

Jane tucked her hand under Elizabeth's arm. "They are young. They cannot help their exuberance. They will mature out of it soon enough."

Elizabeth rolled her eyes but conceded her sister's point. "Let us hope they do it sooner rather than later."

It only took a minute or two for the rest of the Bennet girls to join Lydia and Kitty.

"Good morning, Miss Bennet. Miss Elizabeth. Miss Mary." Mr. Denny bowed to each of the ladies as he greeted them. "I was just telling Miss Katherine and Miss Lydia that I am happy to be in their company once more."

"We are ever so glad you are returned, as well." Lydia fluttered her eyelashes at the captain.

The younger girls spent the next few minutes flirting with Mr. Denny. Elizabeth, Jane, and Mary looked on but their attention was soon drawn away by the arrival of Darcy and his friends. Mr. Madison tipped his hat and rode on, but Darcy and Bingley stopped.

"Miss Bennet!" Bingley swung down from his saddle. "I was just on my way to your house. How fortuitous it is to find you here!" He bowed.

Darcy followed Bingley's lead. Elizabeth smiled up at him as he tied the mare off and joined her on the wooden walkway. "Good morning, sir." As always happened when she was in his presence, her entire focus was her betrothed. She wished he would kiss her, or at least her hand, but she doubted he would, given their location on a public street.

Darcy's lips lifted in a pleased smile. "Good morning."

Across the road, George Wickham exited the inn and began walking toward the other end of town. He paused in front of a shop about half-way up, looking around for his friend. He quickly located the gentleman and took a few more steps down the wooden sidewalk, intending to cross and greet Denny and what looked like a gaggle of beautiful ladies that surrounded him. He was stopped in his tracks, however, when two horses, one of which was ridden by someone he well knew, joined the group. He changed direction and instead backtracked, going up toward the inn but crossing the street at an intersection. Once on the other side, he tucked himself around the corner and leaned on the wall, watching what was happening two doors down.

It looks like Darcy has feelings for the petite brunette, he thought. He snorted to himself. *Not that he would know what to do with her.* He watched closely, memorizing the features of the woman his former friend stood beside. *Well, look at that! I think she likes him! We cannot have that.* He ducked back, out of sight from the high street, when Darcy and his companion mounted their horses and the ladies disappeared into the building they had been standing in front of. *You took your sister and her money from me. Now I will take your lady from you.* As soon as Darcy and his friend had moved away, Wickham emerged from the side street and hailed Denny. *Once I have told her my tale, she will reject you so fast it will make your head spin,* he thought as he joined his compatriot.

~~~***~~~

Later that day, the Bennet family and their guest joined the Phillipses and a few of the other families of the neighborhood for a card party. Knowing how much her nieces enjoyed spending time with the officers, Mrs. Phillips had prevailed upon her husband to issue a general invitation to them all and was delighted when the majority of them presented themselves at her door. George Wickham was among those who took them up on the invitation.

Wickham made sure he was introduced to all the ladies, especially the one who had seemed to catch Darcy's attention. Miss Elizabeth Bennet was, to his mind, a prime article. She had looks and wit and he wondered what his old "friend" had done to catch her attention. Though he wished to engage her in private conversation, or at least what would pass for that in a crowded room, he decided to sit back and observe for a while. Eventually, though, he felt time slipping away and, when he saw her sitting alone late in the evening, he swiftly crossed the room to bow before her.

"How are you enjoying the evening, Miss Elizabeth?"

"I like it very much." She tipped her head toward their hostess. "My aunt loves company and always surrounds herself with the most interesting people in the neighborhood."

"Yes, there is a most fascinating group of people in attendance tonight." He gestured toward the seat beside her. "May I sit?"

"Certainly." She moved over a little to create more space between them. "How do you like our little town?"

"I have only been here a few hours, but so far, I have enjoyed it very much. Everyone has been most welcoming."

Elizabeth smiled. "I am happy to hear it. Have you been a lieutenant long?"

Ah, Wickham thought, *here is my opportunity.* "No," he replied. "I just signed up today. I never considered it before, but I was recently denied a living in the church that was left to me in my godfather's will and needed a manner of supporting myself."

"Oh, how terrible!" Elizabeth's brow creased as she pressed a hand to her heart. "I am sorry that happened to you. Was there no legal recourse you could take?"

Wickham shook his head, donning the saddest look he could manage. "I could not afford representation. It is an expensive thing to sue someone, and my godfather's son is wealthy and powerful, especially in Derbyshire."

Elizabeth shook her head. "I cannot imagine why a gentleman would do something like that to another."

Wickham shrugged. "I believe it to be the result of jealousy. I was old Mr. Darcy's favorite, and his son hated the fact."

Elizabeth gasped. "Darcy! Mr. Darcy denied you this living?"

Wickham smiled to himself. He could feel victory already. "Indeed, he did." He paused. "Do you know Mr. Darcy?"

Elizabeth clasped her hands in her lap. "I do. He is a guest at a local estate. The gentlemen of his party were committed to an event elsewhere or he would be here with us. Only Mrs. Hurst was able to come."

"I am sorry you have been forced to make his acquaintance." Wickham watched her carefully. He could not determine from her countenance or her behavior if he was making the inroads he hoped to, so he decided to go a bit further. "He is an arrogant, haughty fellow and very unpleasant to speak to. It is a shame, because his father was everything amiable." He leaned toward her and lowered his voice. "Do not allow yourself to be alone with him. His family expects him to marry an heiress, but he is not above persuading other women to his bed." He watched as his seatmate clenched her jaw and turned red.

Elizabeth lifted her chin. "I thank you for sharing your story with me, sir." She stood. "I must speak to my sister." She curtseyed before turning on her heel and leaving.

Wickham bowed and watched her walk away. He frowned. He was not at all certain the interview had turned out as he had intended it, because the lady had not reacted as most did. However, his observations of her, limited as they were, had shown her to be genteel and polite, and he assumed she did not wish to make a scene. That did not mean she did not believe what he had told her. He shrugged to himself and joined his fellow officers at the whist table.

From the other side of the room, where she had joined Jane and their friend Charlotte, Elizabeth watched Lieutenant Wickham sit down to play cards. Her brow was creased, the only reflection of the anger she felt.

"Lizzy, are you well?" Jane touched her sister's arm.

Elizabeth spun her head toward her companions. "I am. I apologize for not paying attention."

"I was just asking what you thought of the officers." Charlotte smirked, her head nodding toward the table where Kitty and Lydia were playing Lottery Tickets with Denny and a captain named Carter. "Your youngest sisters seem to have finally been distracted from flirting with them."

Elizabeth glanced toward the indicated game and rolled her eyes. "I am happy to see something pull their attention away." She pressed her lips together and glanced back at the whist table again. "My opinion of the officers has been lowered a little bit tonight."

Jane tilted her head. "How so?"

"Did you see the gentleman who was seated next to me a few minutes ago?" Elizabeth waited until she had acknowledgement from both ladies. "He sat there and told me a wild tale about Mr. Darcy. I do not believe for one minute that my betrothed would do something so atrocious as to deny someone a living that was promised to him."

Jane's brow creased. "He certainly appears to be everything honorable. There must be some mistake at play. Some ... miscommunication."

"I would have to agree, Eliza. Such behavior does not fit the Mr. Darcy we have come to know in the last few weeks. Are you certain he was speaking about the same person?"

Elizabeth shrugged. "He mentioned Derbyshire in his tale, and Mr. Darcy has told me that he has few relations on his father's side of the family and none in his county. His uncle lives full time in London and is a judge. His aunt is married to a gentleman from Lincolnshire. All of his cousins reside with their parents, either in town in the case of his uncle's children, or on their father's estate. Mr. Wickham could only be speaking of my betrothed."

Charlotte glanced at Jane but spoke again

to Elizabeth. "What will you do with this information?"

"I am going to speak to him about it as soon as possible." Elizabeth paused. "I will ask Papa to allow me to take the gig out tomorrow morning. Mr. Darcy often rides out early in the day and I can, perhaps, meet up with him along my route. I know Mr. Wickham's story to be a blatant falsehood, but I cannot in good conscience keep it from Darcy. It would not do for him to hear of it from someone else."

Jane nodded. "I think that is an excellent plan. Information such as that, true or not, can hurt a gentleman's reputation. Mr. Darcy is too good for something like that to happen to him."

At this, Elizabeth's humor overtook her sense of offense. "You only say that because he agreed to marry me so quickly and because you are fond of his friend."

Jane blushed and rolled her eyes, but chuckled along with her sister and friend. "You think that if it makes you happy, Lizzy." She laughed. "Come, let us have a cup of punch and find a fourth for Commerce. Mrs. Hurst does not appear to be engaged at the moment."

Elizabeth agreed, and soon, she and her friends were engaged in a rousing game of their own. As they played, they maintained a lively discussion.

"So, Charlotte, I see that Mr. Madison has

not waned in his attentions to you." Elizabeth raised a brow as she looked at her friend over her handful of cards.

Charlotte blushed and focused her attention on the game, but answered readily enough. "He has not."

Elizabeth's lips twitched. "How do you feel about it?"

Charlotte shrugged and made a show of arranging her hand, moving the cards around multiple times. "I like him very much, but you know as well as I do that it may come to nothing. I will not get my hopes up for anything from him beyond friendship. He may simply be passing time while in the country."

"Mr. Bingley told me he has never seen his friend behave so with any lady." Jane looked from her own cards to Charlotte. "He believes Mr. Madison is well on his way to being in love with you."

Charlotte's blush deepened. She did not reply.

"Oh, come now, Charlotte." Elizabeth lowered her cards to the table, nearly forgetting to keep them hidden in her eagerness to speak. "You know as well as I do that Mr. Madison is a very nice gentleman. He is intelligent and kind." She glanced over her shoulder when the voice of her cousin suddenly rose above the murmur of the other players. "And he is not ridiculous, as is someone else we all know."

Charlotte rolled her eyes, shaking her head when Jane giggled. "He is not ridiculous, I grant you, and I have done my best to make my interest in him known, but I am not convinced of his interest in anything more than a conversation."

"Well, you think that way if it makes you feel better." Elizabeth asked for a card and was given one. "Mrs. Hurst, you are residing in the same house as Charlotte's caller. Do you have an opinion on his interest in her?"

Louisa's eyes widened, as though she was surprised to be addressed, but she smiled. "Mr. Hurst commented just the other day that Mr. Madison seems to be quite enamored of you, Miss Lucas. I am certain your friends are correct and that it is likely he will offer for you before he leaves the area."

"That is good to hear," Charlotte replied. "I confess I hope he does." She leaned forward and lowered her voice. "I like him very much and would be delighted if he were to propose." She leaned back. "What about you, Jane, and your Mr. Bingley?"

Jane sighed. "He is the most amiable gentleman of my acquaintance. I like him very much."

Elizabeth tilted her head and looked at her sister. "Enough to marry him?"

It was Jane's turn to blush. She took a deep breath, looked around as though to make sure no one was listening, and leaned forward. In a soft voice, she replied. "Oh, yes. How can one not fall in love with someone so kind, generous, and handsome?"

Louisa laughed. "He is a charmer, is he not? I hate to tell tales and give away his secrets, but I believe he likes you just as much." She paused, fingering the tops of her cards. "Charles must be cautious in all his dealings at this point. He must be sure of both himself and those around him. I cannot say why." She looked around at her new friends before addressing Jane once more. "In the past, he often acted on the impulse of the moment. It has only been recently, in the last few months, that events have taught him to be more careful and … thoughtful; to consider the consequences of his actions before he moves." She bit her lip. "I wish it did not have to be so. I believe he was happier before. But, it is what it is." She looked up and smiled. "I do not mean to be cryptic. I just wished to assure Miss Bennet that Charles likes her very much but feels that he needs to be certain of himself before he makes any decisions about his future."

"I am happy to hear it. I pray he soon finds the certainty he needs." Jane smiled and played her hand.

Not long after that, the party began to break up. The Bennet ladies made plans with Charlotte and Louisa to get together at Netherfield for tea in a day or two, then they went their separate ways for the night.

~~~***~~~

The next morning, Elizabeth gained her father's permission for the use of his antique carriage. She waited patiently for the groom to hitch the mare to it, then eagerly climbed in and took up the reins. Though she would usually whip Gracie up to a gallop, today she maintained a much slower pace. She headed directly toward the spot she had seen Darcy the last time she and her father took the gig out. Upon reaching the spot, she pulled the horse to a stop and waited, soaking in the quiet of the morning and listening carefully for the sounds of a horse and rider. She was just beginning to think he was not coming when she heard hoof beats approaching. She sighed in relief and, when he got closer, waved at him.

Darcy reined his animal to a canter and then a trot, finally stopping him altogether when he reached the fence that separated the field in which he was riding from the road where Elizabeth was seated. He smiled at her.

"Good morning. Were you waiting for me?"

Elizabeth laughed. "I confess I was. Will you join me?"

Darcy grinned. "I will." With that, he dismounted, tied Apollo off to a fence post, and clambered over the railing, dropping to the ground on the other side. In two steps, he was next to the carriage and climbing up in. After a quick glance up and down the road, he leaned over and brushed his lips over hers. "What a fabulous way to begin a day." He settled back into the squabs and took her hand. "To what do I owe this pleasure?"

Elizabeth was silent for a moment as she stared at him with a smile tipping the corners of her lips up, but then she looked down and sobered. "I wished to tell you something that happened last evening." She bit her lip and brought her gaze up to meet his. "There was a gentleman there, an officer, who said terrible things about you. I know they must be dreadful falsehoods and I do not believe for a second that you are capable of such actions, but I could not rest until you were made aware of them. I fear that your reputation could be tarnished if this man spreads his stories to anyone else, and as Jane pointed out, you are too good and honorable a person to have to go through something like that."

Darcy's brow creased. "Who was this gentleman and what did he say?"

"He was a lieutenant named Wickham." Elizabeth saw Darcy start but pushed forward with her story. She watched his lips press tighter and tighter together and his countenance grow increasingly grim the longer she spoke. When she was finished, she waited in silence as he rubbed his thumb over the back of her hand. Finally, she saw him swallow and he looked into her eyes.

"I am sorry you were subjected to Mr. Wickham's presence. Did he touch you? Did he hurt you at all?"

Elizabeth shook her head. "No, he did not. He maintained a respectable distance, and the only injury I received was the unpleasantness of his speech."

Darcy took a deep breath. "Good." He sighed, looking down at their joined hands, and nodded once. He looked up. "Allow me to tell you my side of the story."

"Please do." Elizabeth smiled encouragingly.

Chapter 10

The corners of Darcy's lips lifted briefly, but his frown returned as he began to speak. "George Wickham was the son of my father's steward and was my father's godson. He was raised by both parents. John Wickham was an excellent estate manager; he and my father held each other in high esteem and great trust. Mrs. Wickham was a spendthrift. I recall my mother once calling her grasping and saying she was reaching far above her position in society. George spent the majority of his time with Mrs. Wickham, though he and I played together frequently.

"George has a way about him that draws people in. He can be very charming when he wishes to be, and after my mother's death, my father drew great comfort from his visits. By that time, Mrs. Wickham had also passed away and since we were playmates, he was often in company with me." Darcy looked down and paused, then took another deep breath, letting it out slowly.

"As I said, Father was very close to the elder Mr. Wickham by this point and trusted him above all others. He wished to honor the man he thought of as a friend by assisting his son. Therefore, he sent George to school with me – we are only a few months apart in age – starting with Eton. In his will, he left his godson a bequest of one thousand pounds, along with the promise of a living that was in his gift, should George take orders.

"You already know that my father died four years ago." He looked up again and, when Elizabeth nodded her understanding, continued. "His steward and friend followed him to the grave barely six months later. It was then that George finally came to me wanting to know if he had been left anything by his godfather. He was disappointed to discover what his bequest was." Darcy glanced up when Elizabeth gasped.

"How ungrateful!" She pressed her lips together. "I am sorry I interrupted you."

Darcy gave her a small smile. "I do not mind." He sighed. "George declared that he had no desire to join the church and since I knew he was unsuitable to lead a congregation, I acceded to his desire to be compensated. We negotiated a bit, and in the end he accepted a sum of three thousand pounds in lieu of the living. He signed away his rights to the position, took his money, and left Pemberley."

Elizabeth's brow creased. "I do not understand; if he agreed to the sum and attached his signature to the acceptance, why is he now saying you deprived him of it?"

"Do you remember when I said he was unfit for the church?"

She nodded. "I do." Her eyes widened. "In what way is he unsuitable?"

"Wickham has always had vicious propensities. He often injured me during our play but always passed it off as an accident, especially in front of his godfather. I remained silent about the events because I had no proof that they had been done on purpose and I saw how much comfort he brought to my only remaining parent." Darcy shrugged. "Once my father had sent us off to school, Wickham fell in with a group of boys whose behavior tended toward wildness. They often pulled pranks on the more studious and quiet of us and generally got away with it. Then, when we moved on to University, George and I grew further apart. He often skipped classes, cheated on exams, and drank himself into a stupor. Worse, we shared an apartment, and more than once, I came home from studying or from class to find he had a woman in his room." Darcy looked up, gazing deep into her eyes. "I never caroused as he did. I decided long ago that I never wished to be tarred with the same brush as he, and have kept myself pure, as I was taught in church to do. I cannot say I have never been tempted. I have. However, I have always removed myself from the situation with alacrity, if not with grace."

Elizabeth felt her heart swell. "Thank you for sharing that part. I am happy to hear it. I know it is not the usual thing for a gentleman. It could not have been easy to avoid the things your classmates participated in."

The corner of Darcy's lip twitched upward. "It was difficult. At times I felt very much alone, though I know I was not, especially when I was much younger. You would be surprised at the young men who declare themselves accomplished with the ladies who have never even been kissed."

Elizabeth giggled behind her hand. "Oh, my."

Darcy chuckled for a moment before becoming serious once more. "I did not hear from Wickham for two years after I paid him for the living." He paused and played with her hand, as though he was uncertain what to say next. "This past summer, he intruded into my life again in a manner that nearly ended in disaster." He looked into Elizabeth's eyes again. "I beg you to keep what I am about to tell you a secret. Will you do that?"

Elizabeth instantly agreed. "Of course." She squeezed his hand.

"I spoke to you of my sister, Georgiana." Elizabeth nodded and he continued. "She was in school in London for a year or two and when she was finished with her studies this past spring, a companion was hired for her. I was persuaded by this woman, Mrs. Younge, to lease a house in Ramsgate for my sister for the summer. I was assured that many of Georgiana's friends and their families would be holidaying there. Since I wished to allow her to have some pleasant company for the season and also wanted to spare her the putrid air of London, I agreed. I happily waved the pair of them off, content in having found a way for my only close family member to have an enjoyable summer.

"Georgiana had not been gone for many days when I began to miss her. I decided to wrap up my concerns in town as soon as possible so I could visit, and I hoped to surprise her." He paused and snorted. "I certainly did that."

Elizabeth squeezed his hand again but said nothing.

"She and Mrs. Younge both reacted very strangely to my arrival. It did not take long before my sister confessed to her reasons." He stopped again, looking over Elizabeth's shoulder. He swallowed. "It turns out, the companion had a previous connection to George Wickham; it had been at his instigation that she approached me to send Georgiana to Ramsgate. Once they arrived, the pair contrived to meet when my sister and Mrs. Younge were out shopping, and from there, Wickham began paying a great deal of attention to Georgiana. Courting her, if you will. Eventually, he convinced my sister that he was in love with her and to elope with him to Gretna Green. He insisted she keep it a secret from me. I had arrived just two days before their planned departure."

Elizabeth's free hand had come up to cover her mouth, which had fallen open. "Thank goodness you visited! What happened after that?"

"I sent a note to Wickham's residence, demanding that he leave. He did, without a word to my sister. She was heartbroken when he would not present himself to me as her suitor. She realized then that he never loved her and was only after her dowry, which is thirty thousand pounds. Mrs. Younge was turned out immediately without a reference. Her things were sent to her later." He paused once more. "Georgiana is in London now, with a new companion whose references were more carefully scrutinized than those of Mrs. Younge had been. She remains melancholy; she has gone from a happy and cheerful girl to a shadow." He sighed. "She is just fifteen, too young to have to suffer such a thing."

"I agree. The poor girl!" Elizabeth rubbed the back of Darcy's hand, which still held one of hers in its grasp. "Mr. Wickham is a liar, then. It is not you who is a rake, it is he. I am so glad I gave his words no credence."

"Thank you for trusting me, and thank you for your compassionate response. Not every lady would." Darcy leaned forward and brushed his lips against hers.

Elizabeth allowed his liberties and they enjoyed a few minutes of stolen kisses before parting. "You will come to Longbourn today?"

"I would not miss it for the world." With a parting caress of his lips, Darcy jumped down out of the curricle and climbed over the fence to his patiently awaiting horse. He mounted and waved before kicking the animal into motion.

Elizabeth watched him ride away and

sighed. She wished their interlude had not had to end, but judging by the location of the sun in the sky, she was out past her time and needed to get home. She expertly turned the equipage around before slapping the reins on Gracie's back and speeding toward Longbourn.

~~~***~~~

True to his word, Darcy arrived at the Bennet home that afternoon, Bingley and Madison in tow. Lady Lucas and her daughters had come for a visit, along with two of her younger sons, making the drawing room a bit tight, but no one seemed to mind, much less the gentlemen. Madison had immediately removed to Charlotte's side, barely paying his respects to the rest of the group. Bingley made a pretty bow and greeted everyone heartily, but then sat himself next to Jane and proceeded to mimic his friend and ignore everyone else in the room. Though he knew he should be ashamed of it, Darcy followed suit, acknowledging everyone properly but then giving over his entire attention to Elizabeth. Mr. Collins, who had spent the first part of the Lucases' visit trying to gain Charlotte's esteem, did his best to interfere with everyone else's conversation while at the same time publicly rebuking his cousin Elizabeth.

"Did you enjoy the remainder of your ride this morning?" Elizabeth lifted a brow and tilted her head as she smirked at him.

"I did. It was quite invigorating." Darcy's lips twitched. "I see that you returned home safely."

"I did." She laughed. "I may have frightened some sheep in the far field, though."

Darcy chuckled. "Did you take a turn too fast?"

Elizabeth blushed. "Something like that." She laughed.

Darcy admired her twinkling eyes for a long moment, but then recalled their conversation of the morning. "I think it would behoove me to speak to your father. Is he available?"

She nodded. "I understand him to be in his book room." She rose. "I will show you the way." Turning toward her mother, she excused herself and Darcy and slipped into the hallway, her betrothed on her heels.

Upon reaching her father's library, Elizabeth knocked on the closed door and leaned her head toward the wooden panel to easier hear Mr. Bennet's response.

"Enter."

She pushed the door open and led Darcy inside. "Papa," she said, "Mr. Darcy has something important to tell you. Would you be willing to listen to him now, or should he wait until after we dine?"

Bennet's brows rose and he leaned forward from where he had slouched as he read. He placed his book on the desk in front of him, pages open and spine up. "Now is as good a time as any." He waved them inside. "Close the door behind you, Elizabeth." He stood and bowed to Darcy. "Have a seat."

"Thank you, sir." Darcy waited for his betrothed to sit; he then followed suit, moving his chair closer to hers.

Bennet smirked when he saw his soon-to-be-son sliding the furniture toward Elizabeth. He clasped his hands and laid them on the desk as he waited for Darcy to begin.

The younger gentleman cleared his throat and glanced at his betrothed before looking back at Bennet. "I understand from Elizabeth that she and her sisters have made the acquaintance of an officer by the name of Wickham, and that this man tried to blacken my name to her."

Bennet's brow creased. "Wickham?" He tilted his head and looked at his daughter. "I do seem to recall Lydia mentioning someone by that name."

Elizabeth nodded. "Yes, she thought he was quite handsome, and until she became distracted with her cards, flirted with him quite a bit last night. Not that she did not flirt with the other officers, as well; she did." She shrugged. "But yes, Lydia was speaking of him last evening upon our return."

"I thought so." Bennet moved his attention back to Darcy. "Do you know this Mr. Wickham, sir?"

"I do." Darcy's mien grew more solemn as

he related to Bennet the tale he had shared with Elizabeth earlier in the day. "I wanted you to be aware of the manner of man he is so you could better protect your daughters, especially the younger ones."

Bennet had leaned back in his chair as Darcy's tale had unfolded, clasping his hands together with index fingers up and pressed to his lips. Now, he moved his hands down. "I thank you for the information. They are silly girls and my wife indulges them."

"Father ..." Elizabeth hesitated but, seeing Bennet's encouraging nod, plunged forward. "I know that you probably think they are not wealthy enough to be a target for someone like Mr. Wickham, but based on what Mr. Darcy has said, the lieutenant does not target only wealthy young ladies. Lydia, especially, is fearless. I can see her being easily persuaded to behave in a manner she should not. After all, if Miss Darcy, who is better educated, fell for the scheme, what is to stop my sister, whose only interest in schooling was to learn to read novels and do household accounts?"

Bennet nodded and sighed. "You do have a point." He thought a bit longer, and neither his daughter nor his future son thought it wise to interrupt. Finally, he sat up again. "I will have to take more time to consider what I wish to do with this information. Something will have to be done to protect the girls; I simply do not know yet what avenue is best."

He stood and held his hand out to Darcy. "I thank you for bringing this to me. I promise you that I will not ignore it."

Darcy bowed. "Thank you for taking it seriously."

"Thank you, Papa." Elizabeth curtseyed to her father. "We will be dining very soon."

"I will be along shortly." Bennet waved toward the door. "Tell your mother to hold the meal until I get to the table."

"Yes, sir." Elizabeth took the elbow that Darcy held out to her and left the room with him.

Chapter 11

The next day, Darcy entered Netherfield's dining room to break his fast just as his host was sitting down to eat.

"Good morning, Darcy! How was your ride?"

"It was quite refreshing, despite not seeing Miss Elizabeth." Darcy filled his plate as he spoke.

"Do you see her often when you are out for exercise?"

Darcy turned toward the table, plate in hand. "Not often, no, but I do occasionally. I saw her yesterday, as a matter of fact, and had a pleasant conversation with her." He set his plate down and pulled out a chair. As he seated himself next to his friend and nodded to the footman holding the coffee carafe, he continued. "She never has Miss Bennet with her; I do not know if she does not wish for her sister to join her in the mornings or if there is some other reason she is alone." He shrugged and picked up a piece of egg with his fork.

Bingley lifted a brow. "I suspect Miss Elizabeth is out before Miss Bennet is even awake. Much like you are always out before I am awake."

Darcy shrugged again. "Perhaps. There is no way to know without asking, though, and I am not about to inquire into the habits of my betrothed's sister."

Bingley laughed. "I completely understand."

Darcy glanced at the door and, seeing that it was closed and the servants were out of the room, leaned closer to his friend. "How goes it with Miss Bennet, anyway?"

Bingley put down his fork. "I am hopeful. I have been subtly questioning her, asking about this person or that that I've seen about the area. Her responses have been all that is kind and generous. I am optimistic that she is everything I hope she is."

Darcy nodded. He swallowed what was in his mouth and took a sip of coffee. "Elizabeth tells me Miss Bennet is incapable of being unkind or cruel. I suspect you will find it to be true."

"I hope so. I pray so."

The gentlemen fell silent for a long moment but then, hearing the noise of the rest of the guests coming toward the room, looked to the door. Seconds later, it opened and the Hursts entered the room, followed by Madison.

"Good morning!" Bingley jumped up and bowed, making an extravagant gesture toward the sideboard. "We started without you, but there is plenty left for your enjoyment."

The entire party laughed as Hurst helped his wife to sit and he and Madison went to fill plates.

Madison brought his breakfast to the table and sat across from Darcy. "How goes it with Miss Elizabeth?"

Darcy could not help the smile that spread across his face. "Very well, thank you. She is everything I ever wanted in a woman."

Bingley laughed. "Besotted, is he not?"

Madison lifted his cup of coffee, hiding a grin. "That, he is."

"You are one to tease." Hurst set a plate in front of Louisa and another at the place next to her. "How goes it with Miss Lucas?"

Madison blushed but one corner of his lips lifted in a slight smirk. "Very well. I think she likes me as much as I do her. She has given me every indication that she would accept my addresses, were I to make them."

"Will you?" Louisa tilted her head as she looked at him. "You are not merely trifling with her, are you?"

"No, Mrs. Hurst, I am not." He glanced around the table at his friends. "I am not one to expose my emotions for all and sundry, but I am certain I can trust everyone in this room; none will repeat what I say." He paused as the other occupants of the room nodded. "I was attracted to her from the first moment I saw her. She is older than the typical lady thrown at my head during the season in town and she is not as beautiful as, say, Miss Bennet, but she is quite pretty. She is sensible, intelligent without being a bluestocking, and good-humored. She makes me forget myself, and, frankly, she takes my breath away. I have no intention of leaving Hertfordshire without her."

Hurst pointed his fork at Madison. "That Mr. Collins does his best whenever they are in company to pull her attention towards him. He is not an unworthy suitor. Perhaps you ought to make your move sooner rather than later."

Louisa set her cup of tea down. "She told me at the card party that she likes you and would accept your addresses, but that she does not believe you are interested in more than friendship while you are here."

Madison sat back, eyes wide. He closed his mouth, which had fallen open. "Well, then, I suppose I should make my intentions clear." He shook his head. "I will call on her today."

Bingley grinned. "Good idea. Nothing like a little direct speech to clear the air."

"Exactly." Madison lifted his fork in the air in salute.

Turning to Louisa, Bingley said, "I am happy that you are making friends here."

"I am, as well." Louisa sighed and smiled. "It is such a relief. I am so glad you encouraged us to come here with you."

"I agree." Hurst gave his attention to his brother-in-law. "I was concerned for her well-being for a while there. Coming to Netherfield has breathed new life into both of us."

"Good. I am glad to hear it." Bingley glanced at Darcy. "I hope to use this time to move on with my life."

Louisa bit her lip. "Miss Bennet seems like a kind and loving person."

"She does." Bingley smiled at his sister. "I was just telling Darcy that I have high hopes in regards to her."

Hurst leaned back in his seat. "So, it seems as though all the single gentlemen of Netherfield may be giving up their bachelorhoods." He looked around at his friends. "It must be something in the air." He winked when the rest of the party laughed.

~~~***~~~

At Longbourn that same morning, the ladies of the house were at home and visiting with the neighbors. Mr. Collins had disappeared early. No one knew where he had taken himself off to, and no one seemed to care.

The officers were among those who made their way into the drawing room, and Elizabeth was dismayed to see Mr. Wickham among them. As far as she knew, her father had yet to say anything to her mother and sisters about the man.

Her greeting to the newest officer was barely civil, and she watched warily as he approached her youngest sister. She vowed to herself to keep an eye on Lydia and to intervene if it seemed necessary. Her attention was diverted from her vigil when she noticed her father enter the room and take a seat in a quiet corner. He had a book in his hand, which he promptly opened, but it appeared to his favorite daughter that he was not really reading it. She relaxed with his presence, and when Mrs. Goulding approached to congratulate her on her upcoming nuptials, Elizabeth was able to smile and give the matron her full attention.

In his chair across the room, Bennet made a show of being involved with his book, but his gaze was rarely on the page. He had seen the officers enter from the drive and approach the house. He knew not which was Wickham, but he intended to find out. He had not yet decided what to do about the man; he hoped that observation would help him decide.

By paying careful attention, he was able to discern which officer was the one who had concerned Darcy so much. It did not take long for him to see that his youngest child was, indeed, enamored of the man. His notice was drawn away when the housekeeper approached him with the information that his steward required his presence. He rose from his chair and, with a long, last, stern look in Wickham's direction, retired to his book room.

Wickham himself had, by this time, become bored with Lydia's ploys for attention. His eyes wandered over the occupants of the room. He noted Elizabeth sitting with her elder sister and two other young ladies. He had been surprised by her cold reception to his greeting when he arrived; he assumed she had decided not to believe his tale about Darcy. He still hoped to discredit the other man, though, and prevent his marriage. He had originally thought to share his story with the youngest Bennet. He had, indeed, spoken of it briefly to her. However, Lydia could think of nothing but Darcy's kissing of her sister in public, so he changed his mind. As he looked around the room now, he noted again how attractive the mistress of the house was, and how eager to gossip she seemed to be. When he walked nearer and heard her complaints to her friend about not wanting Darcy as her son-in-law, he smiled to himself. Here surely was his answer. With that in mind, when her conversation seemed to wane and she rose to see to her other guests, he approached her.

"Mrs. Bennet, how good to see you today." He bowed to her, reaching to take her hand and bestow a barely-there kiss to her fingers.

Mrs. Bennet giggled. "Good morning, Mr. Wickham. I am glad you could come to visit." She batted her lashes at him. "Please, sit beside me. The tea service will be here soon and this is my favorite place to sit while I pour."

"Of course." Wickham smiled broadly as he helped her sit and took his place at her side. When they were comfortable, he complimented her taste in decoration as a way to begin a conversation. Before long, when he realized how flirtatious she was with him, he became excited. *She will do,* he thought. *I can drop whispers in her ear about Darcy and know they will be spread about. And ...* His eyes honed in on her décolletage. *Perhaps I can get a bit more than that. I have always appreciated older women.*

In the corner, Bennet had returned and taken up his chair once again. He did not open his book immediately. Instead, he scanned the room, looking to see who was still in attendance and where they were. He was startled to see Wickham sitting very close to his wife. He became increasingly angry as he watched the pair of them flirting. He could clearly see from the officer's mien and frequent glances at Mrs. Bennet's bosom what was going through his mind. He had never seen his spouse of nearly five and twenty years behaving in such a manner with any man. She had not flirted with *him* in at least a dozen. *What is she thinking?* he wondered. He examined his wife's features and thought he detected admiration for Wickham in her eyes. *Well. We cannot have that!* He thought a while longer, his gaze never straying from his wife and her companion. It occurred to him that he could not remember the last time he had shared a bed with her. *I wonder ... yes, that must be it! She is in need of attention. Well, if she gets that sort of consideration from anyone, it's going to be me! I am quite certain I can still summon charm enough to worm my way into her bed.*

Jealousy now fully filling his heart and with a firm resolution to seduce his wife, Bennet bolted out of his chair and marched across the room to stand in front of Mrs. Bennet. "Wife, I have need of you." He took her hand and lifted her from her seat. Turning to Wickham, he, forgetting his manners in his upset, said, "It is time for you to leave. I require a word with my wife." He bowed. "I trust you to see yourself out." He pulled Mrs. Bennet toward the door by the hand he still held.

"Mr. Bennet," his wife cried as she scurried along behind him, "what are you about? How could you be so abominably rude to one of our guests?"

He stopped in front of the door to his book room and turned to her. "Do not think I did not see your behavior with that Wickham fellow," he hissed as quietly as he could. "In all these years of marriage I have never seen you flirt with another man. It occurs to me that you have forgotten to whom you are wed. I will not be cuckolded." With that, he turned and tugged her into his library. Her silence surprised him, but he did not expect it to last. He pulled her inside and shut the door behind her.

In the drawing room, the sound of the argument the master and mistress were having was quite clear, though the words themselves could not be made out. The guests excused themselves and quietly departed, and the girls scattered to their separate amusements, most outside the house except for Mary, who instead decided this would be a good time to practice the pianoforte. Eventually, her playing was interrupted by the sound of her mother screaming at her father before slamming the book room door and marching upstairs, wailing for her salts. The girls did not see their parents the rest of the day, as both ordered supper trays brought to the room in which they were seated, Mrs. Bennet's going to her chambers and Mr. Bennet's going to his book room.

~~~***~~~

The next morning, the Bennet girls stood in the hall outside the breakfast room, whispering among themselves. Mr. Collins was within, standing over the sideboard, and none of them wished to be in the same room with him, especially not alone. Eventually, they heard their parents' footsteps coming down the stairs. They turned as one and hurried into the room to await their arrival.

A few minutes later, they, along with their cousin, watched with wide eyes as their mother fairly glowed, bestowing adoring looks in their father's direction just about every other minute. What was more shocking in their eyes was that he smiled fondly at her every time he caught one of the looks. The girls ate in silence, watching the exchanges and communicating their wonder with each other with their own looks and head tilts.

Before he left the table after breaking his fast, Bennet loudly cleared his throat, catching the attention of all the ladies of his household. "I am in receipt of some information that has startled and alarmed me about the officers of the nearby regiment." He looked at each girl in turn, as well as his wife. "I was uncertain what to do about it, but upon reflection, I have come to the conclusion that the best way to prevent anything untoward is to refuse them admittance." When Lydia began to protest, he raised his hand. "I am the head of this household and it will be as I say." He looked sternly at his youngest. "Do you understand me?"

Collins could not hold his thoughts in any longer. "I am certain my young cousin will be eager to obey her most esteemed father in this regard." He would have gone on longer, but Bennet cut him off with a sharp hand motion.

Lydia rolled her eyes at her cousin, then pouted, crossing her arms over her chest and glowering at her father, but she replied readily enough. "Yes, sir."

Bennet nodded. "Very good. See that you obey." He looked around the table again. "No officer is to be invited here or allowed on Longbourn property from this moment forth. Disobedience will result in a loss of pin money for the next quarter."

The ladies remained silent. The only sounds to be heard were the servants moving about in other rooms. Even Mr. Collins seemed to be hesitant to say anything.

Bennet nodded. He took a final sip of his

morning coffee and stood. "I will be in my book room if I am needed." He walked to the other end of the table to bestow a kiss upon his wife's lips and then turned toward the door.

Mrs. Bennet watched her husband leave the room with a soft smile on her lips. She sighed before turning to her second daughter and becoming serious. "Lizzy, I would have a word with you." She opened her mouth to speak, but then frowned at her husband's cousin. "Mr. Collins, I require you to leave the room." She waved toward the door. "Perhaps you may visit with my husband in his book room."

"Oh, but Mrs. Bennet, surely you will need my support to lend weight to whatever it is you wish to say to Miss Elizabeth." He gave Lizzy a coy smile. "After all, I am certain that your husband will soon see the wisdom of breaking her engagement to my esteemed patroness' nephew, and then she will be married to me."

Mrs. Bennet gave him a look that her daughters knew well. "Mr. Collins! Leave!"

Collins' eyes widened and he drew his head back. His mouth opened and closed. He swallowed. Then, he stiffened and stood. With a bow, he acquiesced to her desires. "Very well, then." He spun on his heel and left the room.

Mrs. Bennet turned to her second daughter. "I have it on good authority that Mr. Darcy is a heartless scoundrel," she said urgently. "He has ruined several other young ladies; I know you wish for faithfulness in a husband – you have said so repeatedly – and he is clearly not going to be so. I want you to go to your father right now and tell him you wish to break your engagement. Mr. Collins is prepared to marry you. He is a clergyman. He will not break a commandment like that."

Elizabeth was stunned at her mother's words, not because of their content but because the lady was still insisting on having her way. "No, Mama. I will not. I do not know who told you such a thing about Mr. Darcy, but it is not true. He and I have discussed this already. I trust him. Furthermore, I have already told you multiple times that, even if I were to break my betrothal, I would never marry Mr. Collins. He is ridiculous and I cannot respect him."

Mrs. Bennet pressed her lips together momentarily, but then tried again, repeating Wickham's story about the living. She and her second daughter ended in a huge argument, because she would not listen to Elizabeth's insistence that she had heard Darcy's side of the story and trusted him above the lieutenant, and Elizabeth would not even consider jilting her betrothed. Though the other girls sat at first and watched in wonder, their heads bouncing back and forth between mother and sister, they eventually decided, one at a time, that perhaps discretion is the better part of valor and slipped away to gather in a different room.

Chapter 12

Elizabeth's argument with her mother last-
ed for several long minutes, until her father
caught wind of it and returned to the dining
room to put an end to it. She was not certain
what exactly drew him out of his book room.
She thought he might have heard her voice
and decided to rescue her, but it could have
just as likely have been that her mother threw
a few teacups at the wall and it was the shat-
tering of the china that caught his attention.
She shook her head as she tromped up the
path to Oakham Mount. Whichever it was, she
was grateful for his appearance. She hated arguing, especially with her mother, for the
simple reason that it was unladylike. She may
have a fondness for equipages that would rival
the most enthusiastic member of the Four-in-
Hand Club in London, but she was still a gen-
tlewoman and she still wished to behave in a
manner fitting to her status. If her father had
not intervened, she and her mother might still
be screaming at each other like fishwives.

Reaching the top of the rise, Elizabeth seated herself on a boulder that jutted up from
the ground. This was her favorite spot to sit
and think. She could see Longbourn's house
from here, and beyond it, the church that was
part of the estate. She had a good view of the
stables and paddock, and the fields beyond.
In the distance, she could see small dark dots

that were the tenants going about their duties on their farms. She drank her fill of the view and then closed her eyes and whispered a quick prayer, asking for forgiveness for losing her temper and being disrespectful to her mother. Peace enveloped her, and she opened her eyes again, thinking about what Mrs. Bennet had said.

It was clear to her that, despite her father's directive that her mother cease all attempts at breaking up her betrothal to Darcy, Mrs. Bennet was choosing not to obey. *Clearly, Mr. Wickham told her his story yesterday,* Elizabeth thought. *I wondered what he was doing sitting with her like that.* She removed her bonnet, tying the ribbons and looping them over her arm. She took a deep breath and let it out slowly. Then, clasping her hands together around her knees, which she had drawn up to her chest, she allowed her eyes to wander over the view once more. She noticed riders approach the house and knew they were probably Darcy and Bingley. She thought she should perhaps head home but knew that Jane would tell the gentlemen where she had gone and her betrothed would soon seek her out. Not two minutes passed before her prediction came true. She saw Darcy exit the house and mount his gelding. She waited patiently, enjoying the sun that warmed the stone on which she sat, despite the cool air.

"Are you well, my love?" Darcy lowered

himself to the boulder beside her and leaned over to caress her lips with his before pulling back to examine her features closely. "Jane told me what happened and where I would probably find you." He lifted an arm over her head, settling his hand on her shoulder and pulling her close.

"I am better now than I was a few minutes ago." Elizabeth smiled at him and leaned her head against his shoulder. "I would rather not talk about it, though; at least, not right now."

Darcy kissed the top of her head. "Then, I will not ask." He ran his hand up and down her arm. "I am sorry your day has begun so poorly."

Elizabeth sighed. "Thank you. I suppose I should have seen it coming."

"What do you mean?"

She explained to him the events of the previous day. "I am concerned about what he might do now. After all, he has spoken to both me and my mother in an effort to break us up. What if he speaks to others in the area? He can be quite charming; what if the neighbors believe him? Too, my father has banned all officers from Longbourn. What will Mr. Wickham do in response to that?" She looked into Darcy's eyes, and he could read the anxiety in hers.

"I am not at all worried about Wickham trying to ruin my reputation. He has spread his stories all over England." Darcy shrugged. "I will not defend myself to those who judge without knowing all the facts. I cannot without exposing my sister and that I will not do."

"I know, and I do not wish for that. I feel it is unfair, though, for you to be drawn as a black-hearted villain when you are not." She kissed his jawline and then lifted her face to accept his kiss in return.

"Life is not fair, my love. These things happen." He paused. "As for his reaction to your unbelief of his tales and his banishment from Longbourn, your father banned all officers, not just Wickham. I doubt he takes it personally, at least not as far as you are concerned. I will write to my cousin, though, and see if he cannot find a position for him somewhere far away from here."

Elizabeth nodded. She thought a moment, and then said, "I am certain my mother will spread what he told her all over Meryton. She is unstoppable when she has gossip to share. I apologize for that."

Darcy squeezed her shoulder again. "There is no need. There are gossips everywhere and at all levels of society. I would be surprised if she did not share it. We will deal with any repercussions as they happen."

"Thank you. I do wish she would keep it to herself, though."

"So do I, my dear, but it is of no consequence if she does not." Darcy was silent for a while but then changed the subject. "Why did you not drive the curricle when you needed time alone?"

"Papa does not allow me to drive when I am upset. He says it leads to poor decisions. He knows walking also helps me to settle my mind and emotions and he urged me out of doors but sent word to the stables that I was not allowed to take the gig." Elizabeth snuggled closer to her betrothed as she spoke.

"That is wise." He thought about the times he had gone for a ride to do the same and how he had taken a few tumbles because of his recklessness. He shuddered to think what could happen to his Elizabeth if she were driving in such a state. The wind suddenly picked up, becoming sharper and colder.

"Come," he said, "it is far too cold to be sitting up here. Let me take you back to Longbourn. Bingley and I planned to stay the day; you can entertain me for a while and save your poor father from having to do so."

Elizabeth laughed at his words. She accepted his hand to help her stand and then jump off the rock. "He is more likely to need rescuing from Mr. Collins than from you. I do not believe he would mind your presence in his library."

~~~***~~~

An hour or two later, Elizabeth and her sisters were sitting in the drawing room completing various projects they had recently begun. Darcy and Bingley had joined Mr. Bennet in his book room, partially to blunt the effect of

Collins' presence and partly because their company was pleasant for the elder gentleman. Mrs. Bennet had retired to her rooms after her argument with her second daughter and was not expected below stairs until at least time to dine.

Kitty jumped up. "I think I hear a carriage!" She leaned against the window. "I do! It is huge! I wonder who it could be?"

"Well," Lydia remarked, "at least it cannot be Mr. Collins, since he is already here."

The other girls giggled but rushed to put their things away. They then sat and composed themselves, their hands clasped in their laps, shoulders back, and spines straight.

"Lady Catherine de Bourgh to see you, Miss Elizabeth." Mrs. Hill made the announcement before curtseying and leaving the room.

"Which of you is Miss Elizabeth Bennet?"

Elizabeth had been surprised to hear the name of the visitor. She examined the older lady with the grey hair and pompous demeanor and wondered what Darcy's aunt could want with her. She stepped forward. "I am she." She curtseyed. "Welcome to Longbourn."

Lady Catherine lifted her chin, looking down her nose at Elizabeth. "I am here to have a word with you." She glanced around at the other young ladies, a severe look on her face. "In private."

Elizabeth hesitated. She did not wish to speak in confidence to this woman, but neither did she want to expose her sisters to any more disdain than they had already experienced. She opened her mouth to invite her to walk in the garden when the sound of thunder rumbled through the windows and a heavy rain began beating on the glass. She sighed to herself.

"Lizzy." Mary approached and put her hand on her older sister's arm. "Perhaps you can take your guest to the back parlor. It is quiet back there and the book room is nearby, in case you need anything."

Elizabeth understood what her sister was telling her: her betrothed and her father were both a few steps away, should she need assistance. She nodded. "What an excellent idea, Mary. Thank you." She smiled, pressing her hand on the younger girl's before turning to her guest. "If you will follow me, madam."

A minute later, the pair of them were ensconced in the empty room, alone. Lady Catherine turned to Elizabeth.

"You can be at no loss, Miss Bennet, to understand why I have traveled here to Hertfordshire."

Elizabeth's eyes widened and her brows rose. "Indeed, I do not understand. What is your purpose in visiting Longbourn, a home you have never before entered, and asking to speak to me instead of one of my parents?"

Lady Catherine's eyes narrowed. Her lips compressed to a thin line and remained that way for half a minute before she opened them again. "I am not to be trifled with! As insincere as you appear to be, you will not find me so. I have been told that you, Miss Elizabeth Bennet, upon whose cousin this home has been entailed, are engaged to my nephew, Mr. Darcy."

Before Elizabeth could reply, the door burst open and Mr. Collins rushed in. He bowed before the visitor. "Lady Catherine, what a surprise! I am sorry I was not able to receive you as soon as you entered the house." He turned an accusing eye on his cousin. "I was not immediately made aware of your entrance. I heard your voice and hurried to attend you."

Lady Catherine looked at her rector and sniffed. "I came to speak to Miss Bennet and do not require assistance. You may, however, remain." She turned once more toward Elizabeth. "As I was saying, I have it on good authority that you have engaged yourself to my nephew. Though I knew it must be a malicious falsehood, I immediately came here to make my sentiments known."

"I cannot imagine how you would have heard about any betrothal of mine. We have no prior acquaintance."

"I wrote to her, Cousin Elizabeth. It-"

Lady Catherine cut Mr. Collins off as though he had not spoken at all. "Impertinent girl! What if I were to tell you that you cannot be engaged to him, because he is promised to my daughter? What do you say to that?"

Elizabeth shrugged. She was the picture of indifference, though she was beginning to seethe inside. She unclenched her jaw long enough to reply but the rest of her body was held tightly. "If that is so, you cannot suppose him to have proposed to me. Do you believe him to be so dishonorable?"

"Cousin! You should not-" Again, Mr. Collins' words were cut off by those of his patroness.

"He is not dishonorable in the least, but you, with your arts and allurements, may have turned his head and made him forget what he owes to his family and his duty."

Elizabeth scoffed at her adversary's words. "Arts and allurements? What arts and allurements? He compromised me, not the other way around."

At that, Lady Catherine began to abuse Elizabeth most abominably. Mr. Collins was not shy about joining his voice to hers, and the volume of their voices became quite high.

For her part, Elizabeth refused to partake in a second row, considering how closely this one followed the one she had with her mother earlier in the day. She stood with arms crossed and lips pressed together, waiting for the pair to wind down so she could dismiss them. A single sudden, loud word stopped them in their tracks.

"Enough!"

Darcy strode into the room, placing himself between Elizabeth and his aunt.

147

"Who do you think you are to enter a home where you are unknown and abuse a daughter of the house?" Darcy's fists were clenched and resting on his hips. His brows were drawn together over his eyes, a deep crease between them.

"I have been informed by my rector that you have engaged yourself to this ..." Lady Catherine waved her hand in Elizabeth's direction. "Person. I have come to put a stop to it. You have been engaged to Anne since your infancy. You will denounce this woman and come with me to town. We will purchase a special license and you and my daughter will marry immediately."

"I will not." Darcy's fists came off his hips to hang straight by his side. "I have told you before, many times before, that I will not marry my cousin. I was not telling a falsehood when I said it. I love Miss Elizabeth Bennet, she has agreed to be my wife, and I will have her and no other. I would rather live the rest of my life alone and leave Pemberley to a stranger than to marry anyone but her." When his aunt began to speak again, he cut her off, making a gesture with his hand. "I do not want to hear it. You will leave this house at once. When you have gained control of your senses once more, you will apologize to Miss Elizabeth and to me."

"Mr. Darcy, surely-"

"And take him with you," Darcy said with a wave of his hand toward Collins. "Lest I make his life as miserable as he has made my Elizabeth's."

Though the lady protested mightily, Darcy touched her elbow and guided her to the door, escorting her through the house without a word. Elizabeth followed and watched as he spoke quietly to his aunt before assisting her into her carriage. He gave Collins a stern look, and the clergyman hustled up the step and into the equipage. Darcy closed the door and called to the coachman to move on.

When his aunt's barouche box had pulled out of the gate, Darcy turned to Elizabeth. He held his hands out to her, and she took them with her own.

"I apologize for my aunt. She had no right to speak to you in such a rude manner." He shook his head. "She has always gotten away with doing such things for the simple reason that she is the daughter of an earl. She has forgotten what simple kindness is, if she ever even learned it."

Elizabeth squeezed his hands. "It is well. I refused to engage in a second argument in one day, so I intended to let her go on until she wore herself out." She sighed. "I have had enough quarrels for one day."

Darcy's thumbs caressed the backs of her hands. "No doubt." He looked over her shoulder. "I need to apologize to your father, as well, and I would rather get it over with now than to wait. Do you mind?"

"Not at all." Elizabeth turned, tucking her hand in the crook of his elbow as he joined her on the top step. She smiled up at him and allowed him to escort her into the house. When she reached the drawing room, she let him go, watching as he approached her father's book room.

Chapter 13

William Collins did his best to soothe his patroness on the short ride from Longbourn to the inn in Meryton. He had been quite put out when Mr. Bennet had ordered him from the library, but his offense had turned to shocked surprise when he heard Lady Catherine's voice coming out of a nearby room. He had done his best to support her in her efforts to make Cousin Elizabeth see reason and give up Mr. Darcy. *The poor man must have been completely enticed by her,* Collins thought. *I cannot imagine he would behave so toward his nearest relation if he had not.* His attention was pulled away from his inner contemplations by the slowing of the carriage. He listened as Lady Catherine instructed her coachman to go into the inn and secure rooms for her.

"You will come inside with me, Mr. Collins. I have a task for you to accomplish." The lady glanced out the windows on both sides. "It would not do to speak of it here; we do not know who might be listening."

Collins bobbed his head and assured her he was her servant, but his brow creased. *What could she have to say that anyone could not hear?*

It took only a few minutes for the driver to come back and help Lady Catherine descend. Collins followed her into the inn and up the stairs to a suite of what appeared to be the best rooms they had. He watched as the servant carried her valise into the bedchamber that connected to the sitting room he stood in. A maid from the inn waited for the groom to leave before entering the bedchamber to do her work, leaving the door open as she did so. When the room was silent, Lady Catherine called him to the window, where she had seated herself in a chair at the small table that sat there. She looked around and when she spoke, her words were quietly said.

"You wrote to me that my nephew had publicly compromised this Bennet girl?"

Collins' head began to bob vigorously. "He did. He walked right up to her in front of everyone and kissed her in a most unseemly manner. Why, I have never-"

Lady Catherine interrupted him. "Keep your voice down." She looked around again. "I want that betrothal broken up. You are to imitate Mr. Darcy. I want you to compromise Miss Elizabeth Bennet more thoroughly than he did. I care not how you accomplish the matter, but I want my nephew to be left with a great disgust of her, so great that he jilts her. You will then marry her. I will pay for a license so that it can be accomplished quickly." Her gaze drilled into her rector. "Do you understand what I am telling you?"

"I, I do. But ... I am a clergyman ..."

"Mr. Collins." Lady Catherine's voice rang

with authority, making him straighten his posture and pay close attention. "Your position is dependent upon me. You will do as you are told."

Collins' lips flapped in silence for a full minute as he tried to both process what she said and form a reply. "My living cannot be stripped from me. It is a life appointment."

She leaned forward. "Indeed. However, I can make your life miserable, and I promise you I will. For the rest of your days." She glared at him.

Collins swallowed. "Yes, ma'am."

Lady Catherine leaned back again. "You understand your assignment, do you not? You are to compromise your cousin, completely and utterly and as publicly as possible, so that my nephew breaks his engagement with her."

"Compromise her ... completely, utterly, publicly ... yes, Lady Catherine." He swallowed. It did not feel quite right, but what was he to do? She held his future felicity in her hands. Elizabeth's pretty face and comely figure flashed in his mind. The thought of having her to wife as he had been fighting to have for weeks now made the task he was assigned seem less onerous.

"When do you plan to do this?"

Collins thought as quickly as he could. "There is to be a ball Wednesday next," he confidently informed her. "I know of no other amusements between now and then. It will be the most public place I can find to do as you ask."

153

Lady Catherine nodded. "Very well. I will return to Rosings in the morning. I will expect a report from you no later than the day after the ball. Send it express." She stood, and her rector stumbled to his feet beside her. "You are dismissed."

"Yes, Lady Catherine." Collins bowed and backed out of the room, continuously praising his patroness and everything about her he could think of until the door finally closed.

Lady Catherine resumed her place at the table the moment the wood panel shut and turned to stare out the window.

In the bedchamber, the maid, Alice, stood wide-eyed out of sight of the sitting room. She had been working steadily but quietly and had not been able to avoid overhearing every word the obviously wealthy lady had said to the strange clergyman. She bit her lip. Her father was a tenant at Longbourn and the eldest Bennet girls had always been kind and generous to those in lower circumstances. They were well thought of by all the tenant families and by most of the shop keepers. She could not allow a stranger to interfere with Miss Elizabeth's life. She knew what she must do. Straightening her shoulders, she left the bedchamber and slipped into the hallway. She could not leave until her shift was over, but that meant she had hours to figure out how to accomplish it.

Later that evening, after the rush of supper

customers and the last of the post coaches had come and gone for the day, Alice approached her employer to ask permission to complete a personal task. She was a responsible girl and never one to ask for time off, and there were enough other maids to cover her duties, so the innkeeper granted her request. She pulled on her cape and bonnet and headed down the road toward Longbourn. She was nearly to the gate when she saw two gentlemen riding toward her from the house. She stopped at the side of the road. As she examined their features in the dimming light, she realized that one of them was Darcy.

"Excuse me, sir." She could hear the nervousness in her own voice. "Might I speak with you?"

The gentlemen pulled their horses to a stop beside her.

"You may, yes." The darker of the two spoke.

She swallowed and then took a deep breath. "Might you be Mr. Darcy?"

Darcy's brows rose. He nodded. "I am."

Alice bobbed her head and swallowed her nerves. "My name is Alice Chamberlain, and I am a maid at the Rosebud and Saber. I was assigned to tend to a lady who took a room for the night. She was with a gentleman and gave him some instructions about Miss Elizabeth. I was on my way to Longbourn to warn her, but perhaps you might do it for me?" A sudden thought made her eyes go wide. "I did not listen on purpose, I swear. I was working in the bedroom and they were in the sitting room and, well, the lady's voice carries."

She saw Darcy's brow crease and watched as he glanced at his friend. He dismounted.

"This lady ... what did she look like? And the gentleman; can you describe him, as well?"

"I can. The gentleman wore a collar like the rector here at the Longbourn church does. The lady was dressed very fine. She was older, about the age of my grandmother, I would think, and *she* just turned sixty. She had gray hair and a severe look about her. She is used to giving commands, I think."

"That sounds like my aunt. Did you hear any names?"

Alice nodded, though she wasn't certain he could see it in the gathering darkness. "She called the gentleman Mr. Collins."

Darcy sighed. "I thought that is what you would say." He paused. "First, do not fret about overhearing anything. The lady was undoubtedly my aunt, and her voice is generally rather loud. Mr. Collins is the rector to whom she has given a living. What did she say to him to bring you all the way out here to Longbourn?"

Alice proceeded to relate everything she had heard. She was glad she had, for it relieved her of a great weight. "Miss Elizabeth does not deserve such treatment as the lady seems to wish for her to receive. I had hoped to warn her to be on her guard."

"You did very well. I thank you for taking the time to tell us." Darcy pressed a coin into her hand. "Would you like an escort back to town? It is rather late to be walking all the way out here."

"My father is a tenant here at Longbourn. His house is not far ... the first one past the turn to Oakham Mount. I often walk home after dark and to work before the sun rises. I will be well on my own, but thank you." Alice dipped a curtsey. Darcy made her feel like a fine lady with his concern for her well-being. It was a feeling she would cherish. "Miss Elizabeth is a lucky lady to have found a gentleman as kind as you to marry her."

Darcy's teeth flashed white as he grinned. "Thank you, Miss Chamberlain. I consider myself the lucky one to have earned her love." He bowed. "Have a good night."

"Good night, sir." She turned and began walking toward her father's home.

~~~***~~~

"Well," Bingley said, blowing out a breath. "What do you think of that information? Will you do anything about it?"

Darcy had by this time remounted his gelding. He nudged Apollo into motion. "I believe her. My aunt would do anything to get her way in the matter of my marriage. She will not dirty her own hands, of course, but she likes to throw her weight around. And Collins appears to me to be the type to do what he is told, when he is told it." He grew quiet for a few minutes. "I hesitate to speak in public, as it were. Let me think about it while we ride and I will share my thoughts when we get back to Netherfield."

"Very good. I am eager to hear them."

~~~***~~~

The next day, Elizabeth, Jane, and Charlotte were admitted to Netherfield by the housekeeper, Mrs. Nichols. She led them to the drawing room, where Louisa Hurst was sitting with her stitching in her hand.

Louisa quickly rose, dropping her needlework on the table beside her chair. "Welcome to Netherfield!" She curtseyed. "I am so happy to see you!" She gestured to a seating area near the fire. "Please join me."

"Charlotte came to Longbourn this morning and we decided we simply could not wait to visit you." Elizabeth settled on the edge of a settee and clasped her hands in her lap. Leaning forward, she lowered her voice a little but not so much that her friends could not all hear. "Of course, you do have three unattached gentlemen here with you, but we thought we could bear their presence well enough." She leaned back, grinning as all three of her companions burst into laughter.

"They certainly are a trial sometimes." Louisa laughed. "I am happy you were able to overlook the presence of the gentlemen to visit. To be honest, I am surprised they have not presented themselves at your homes already."

"I believe Mr. Bingley said something about coming to Longbourn later in the day," Jane said. "Mama will surely ask him to stay to dine with us. Perhaps you and Mr. Hurst could come, as well? My mother does so love to entertain."

Louisa glanced out the window. "I will ask Mr. Hurst what he thinks, but he will want to keep an eye on the weather. He said this morning that the clouds looked ominous."

Elizabeth nodded. "They do. It was sprinkling a little on the way here." She looked out the window briefly. "At least we brought the carriage. If it does begin to downpour, we will be dryer than if we had to walk."

"Lizzy and her walking." Charlotte's tease made her companions laugh. "I am only happy that we brought a proper carriage and not your father's gig."

Elizabeth blushed a little but lifted her chin. "I would have gotten us here much faster in the curricle." She lowered her face and grinned. "But you are correct; we are much dryer in the carriage."

Just then, the housekeeper and a maid brought in the tea service and laid it out in front of Louisa. She began to prepare the teapot as she continued to speak to her guests. She did not get far, though, before all four gentlemen in residence appeared at the door.

"I thought I heard voices!" Bingley hastened across the room, pulled a chair over next to Jane, and sat in it.

"I did, as well, and I was certain the laugh of my favorite lady had reached my ears." Darcy bowed in front of his betrothed, taking her hand and caressing the fingers with his lips.

Elizabeth smiled at him. "I am very happy to see you. Will you join me?" She indicated the space beside her.

"Indeed, I will." Darcy immediately accepted her invitation, flipping the tails of his coat up as he sat.

The rest of the gentlemen joined their favorite ladies and conversations erupted all around. Louisa passed around the tea and cakes with her husband's help, and the eight of them passed an enjoyable quarter hour. Soon, though, Jane rose.

"We promised Mama that we would not be long, and it looks like it has finally begun to rain."

The single gentlemen protested, but Jane would not be moved, and both Elizabeth and Charlotte supported her. Giving in, Darcy and his friends escorted their ladies to the door and helped them with their gloves, bonnets, and coats, at least one of them stealing a surreptitious kiss or two as they did so. Then, they led them out the door and down the steps, finally handing them up into the carriage. They watched it go with matching forlorn looks.

Jane and Elizabeth dropped Charlotte off at Lucas Lodge and then headed home. They had not gone more than a quarter mile before the rain, which had until then been no more than a light drizzle, began to fall in earnest.

Chapter 14

To the dismay of nearly everyone in the vicinity, the heavy rain persisted right up until dawn the day of the ball. Only the heartiest of servants left either Netherfield or Longbourn, and that only if there was a list of essential items that needed purchased or important tasks that needed completed. Darcy and Bingley were forced to stay away; the roads were nearly impassable during such heavy and prolonged rains.

During those three or four days of deluge, Longbourn's heir apparent was remarkably quiet. Lydia was the first to remark on it about halfway through the second day.

"Mr. Collins has been oddly silent, do you not think?"

"Shh, Lydia." Elizabeth shot a look at the door. "Keep your voice down; he will hear you!"

"La! What do I care? He is strange on a good day, but since Lady Catherine was here, he has been behaving more strangely than usual." Lydia shivered. "Not that I am complaining about the quiet. I would rather he were that than to preach at us."

"I agree with Lydia." Kitty looked up from her watercolors. "His manner has been quite different the last few days. I cannot make him out."

"Yes, he is behaving in quite the unusual manner." Mary paused in her writing. "I do not like his usual comportment. It is not right for a clergyman to think so highly of himself. His humility is a false one. I find I much prefer his new behavior." She looked up to find her sisters staring at her. "What?"

Elizabeth shook her head. "Sometimes your insights take me by surprise, Sister. I am only taken aback."

"Oh." Mary looked around at the other three girls. She shrugged, made a face, and then turned her attention back to her extracts.

Jane cleared her throat. "Mr. Collins may have things on his mind. We should not judge him without knowing all the facts."

"Oh, Jane." Lydia sighed as she flounced from the window to a chair. "I knew you would say something like that."

Elizabeth turned her head toward her book in an effort to hide the smirk that twisted her lips.

"You sound like Lizzy," Kitty cried.

Elizabeth could hold her laughter no longer, and soon, her sisters joined her in merriment.

~~~***~~~

Finally, the day of the ball came, and with it the sunshine. The ladies of Longbourn spent the day readying themselves and their gowns. Baths were taken, hair was washed, dried, and styled, and final touches were added to their attire. The entire house was in a fever of excitement. Private balls were rare in their experience, and none had been thrown at Netherfield in at least two decades, possibly three.

Eventually, day turned into evening and the Bennets set off for the Bingley residence, Bennet and Collins in the gig and the ladies in the carriage.

Darcy and Madison were in a drawing room, watching out the window for the arrival of their ladies.

Madison glanced at his friend. "Would you have believed, when you accepted Bingley's invitation, that you would find love in Hertfordshire?"

Darcy shook his head before turning to address the other gentleman. "No, I would not have. In fact, I would have laughed at the notion." He shrugged. "And yet, here I am, waiting for the woman of my dreams to arrive at a ball held largely in our honor."

Madison chuckled. "Here you are." He paused. "What would your father have thought of Miss Elizabeth?"

"He would have loved her." Darcy gave a firm nod of his head but then sighed and looked out the window. "Eventually, anyway. To be honest, I am uncertain how he would have felt. He made it clear I was to marry for love, but he also seemed to think a woman of the *ton* would be my choice. Elizabeth is decidedly not." He turned to his friend. "What about you? What would your father have thought of Miss Lucas?"

"He would have been delighted with her."

Madison leaned against the frame of the window opposite of where Darcy did the same. "My mother is the daughter of a clergyman, you know."

Darcy's brows rose. "I did not know that. Your grandfather did not object?"

"Oh, he did. Most vociferously, as I understand it. However, my father was firm in his desires and would not be moved. Grandfather even threatened to disown him, but he stood his ground and eventually, Grandpapa gave in and allowed the marriage."

Darcy tilted his head and studied the other man. "How did he treat her after that? And, what about the rest of the family?"

"I guess he was rather cold to her until I was born, at which time she became one of his favorite people." Madison shook his head and looked down. "The rest of the family accepted Mama to different degrees. Some became close to her and others did not. She has always said she paid no mind to the opinions of people so wholly unconnected to her."

Darcy laughed. "Elizabeth has said that, as well."

"Your Elizabeth reminds me very much of my mother. I think you will do well together."

Darcy looked down as though embarrassed. "Thank you." He looked up again. "Did you visit Lucas Lodge the other day?" When his friend nodded, he asked, "What happened?"

Madison looked at his glass as he swirled

the red liquid around. "I asked Charlotte for a courtship. She agreed."

"A courtship?" Darcy's brows shot up. "Not an offer of marriage?"

"Not yet. It will come, I promise you. I wanted to wait a little bit to propose. If she did not realize I was interested in her, she would not believe my words of love or that an offer of my hand was sincere. I must do a better job of wooing her." Madison's lips quirked up at one corner.

Darcy snorted. "I suppose you are correct." He held out his hand. "Congratulations for making it so far."

Madison laughed and slapped him on the back. Then, he changed the subject. "Do you think this plan of yours to protect Miss Elizabeth will work?"

"I hope so. I intend to stay close to her the entire night. If I give Collins no opportunity to get near her, I should be able to prevent anything untoward happening." Darcy shifted his shoulder against the window frame. "Your offer of support is much appreciated, as is that of Bingley and his brother. I think Hurst is taking great enjoyment in coming up with ways to keep Elizabeth's cousin away from her."

Madison laughed again. "I believe you are correct. Who would have thought he had it in him?"

Darcy grinned but then glanced out the window again. He suddenly straightened, spun around, and rushed to the door with Madison on his heels. Though he had to fight his way through the crowd, Darcy soon found himself outside and at the bottom of the steps, face to face with the woman who had captured his heart.

"Elizabeth." He bowed to her, kissing her gloved hand.

"Good evening, sir." Elizabeth's lips twitched as though she wanted to laugh. "I am happy to see you so soon."

"I have awaited your arrival with bated breath," Darcy replied. "I wonder now why that was." He winked when she burst out laughing. He bowed to her father, who was standing behind her and listening in with apparent enjoyment, then tucked her hand under his arm and escorted her up the steps and into the house.

"I intend to remain close to you all evening," he said quietly to her as he helped her with her coat.

Elizabeth smiled up at him. "That is lovely, but should you not dance with some of the other ladies? At least with Mrs. Hurst and Jane?"

Darcy paused. He knew she was correct, and he further was aware that his friends would be watching out for her, as well. "I will dance with my hostess and with each of your sisters, but I will endeavor to be near you even when dancing with others."

Elizabeth tilted her head, brow creased. "Do you have a concern about me?"

"No, no." Darcy quickly reassured her. He leaned closer to her ear. "I do not trust your cousin; he does not seem to have given up in his quest for you and I fear he may attempt to harm you or your reputation tonight. It is my desire to protect you from him."

"Oh." For a long moment, Elizabeth stared at him with wide eyes. Finally, she relaxed and gave him a tentative smile. "Very well, then. That is a perfectly reasonable explanation and I accept it. Thank you for explaining it to me."

"Anything for you, my dear." Darcy kissed her hand. "Go ahead and join your sisters in the other room. I will wait here for you. I am eager to see what slippers you chose to go with your gown." He laughed at the strange look that passed over his beloved's face.

"I will be right back." Elizabeth raised her brows but did not reply, instead slipping into the ladies' retiring room to remove her pattens and freshen up.

A few minutes later, Darcy led his betrothed through the receiving line.

"I should have had you join us!" Louisa put her hands to her cheeks. "It never occurred to me. Do forgive me!"

"Do not worry," Elizabeth said. "Mr. Darcy does not like being the center of attention, and I am sure my mother will want to host an evening to honor us a few days before our wedding. We will enjoy simply being guests tonight." She glanced into the ballroom, which could be seen through the open set of double doors. "You have decorated beautifully."

"Thank you." Louisa smiled. "The staff did the work, of course, but I borrowed some of the ideas from other balls I have attended."

"I never would have guessed! I will have to remember some of them for when Mr. Darcy and I host a ball one day." Elizabeth giggled when Darcy's groan filled the air.

"Please, let us marry before we worry about that." Darcy shook his head at his future wife. He rolled his eyes when she continued to laugh, then turned to his hostess. "I agree with Elizabeth; Netherfield has never looked as lovely. You have turned the entire house into an enchanting wonderland." He bowed. "I promised my betrothed to dance with you. Do you have a set free?"

Louisa smiled. "I believe I have the third set free, and I would be happy to offer it to you. Hurst and my brother have claimed the first two already, but I suspect your first set is spoken for, anyway." She laughed when his countenance brightened.

"Yes, it has been claimed already. My beautiful wife-to-be will be my first partner. I accept your third, Mrs. Hurst." He glanced behind him. "I am holding up the line; forgive me. We will see you later."

Darcy led Elizabeth away, into the glittering ballroom. They began to stroll around the perimeter of the large chamber, greeting acquaintances and taking in the decorations. Not long after, they were joined by Charlotte and Mr. Madison. The four took up a place in a corner and talked among themselves while the rest of the guests filtered into the room. Jane approached after having spoken to some friends, and joined the conversation. The orchestra began tuning their instruments and warming up on a dais set up nearby.

"Lizzy." Jane turned to her sister. "Did you see Susannah Long's gown? From the back, I thought she was you. It is nearly the same color, and your hair is styled identically!"

"Is it?" Elizabeth began searching the ballroom with her eyes, trying to locate the other girl. When she did, her mouth formed an O. "You are right! I wonder how that happened? Surely, Mrs. Mallory would have told her that my gown was in the same style."

"Oh, but we remade these gowns. It is possible that she forgot or that it was so long ago that no one thought it would matter."

"I suppose you are correct about that, as well." Elizabeth shrugged. "Oh, well. There is nothing to be done about it now."

Just then, Bingley and the Hursts entered the room. The doors were closed, and the three made their way to the far end. Bingley approached and collected Jane, and his friends and their ladies followed him to the center of the room, where Louisa and Hurst stood waiting. Other couples began to join them, making two lines, and finally, Louisa called the first dance.

Darcy did his best to divide his attention between Elizabeth and his endeavor to keep Collins in his sight at all times. His betrothed, he noted, did not appear to be upset with him for his frequent lapses. When they came together near the end of the first dance of the set, he thought it behooved him to make certain.

"Are you well?"

Elizabeth smiled. "I am. I understand why you are distracted. I appreciate your protection."

Darcy breathed a sigh of relief. He smiled back at her. "Good."

"Where is he?"

The dance separated them for a few minutes, but when they came back, he gave her his reply. "He is dancing with Miss Mary. They are three or four couples down the line."

As she danced, Elizabeth looked past Charlotte, the Longs' eldest niece, and the Gouldings' oldest daughter to see her next younger sister. She then looked across to the other line where Collins stood, his mouth in constant motion. She shuddered. Looking up to her partner, she said, "I love my sister, but better her than me."

Darcy chuckled. "I am happy to hear it." He looked down the row again before turning his attention back to his betrothed. "She would not accept him, would she? If he were to turn his attention from you to her?"

Elizabeth's head began to shake. "Oh, no. I do not think so. From what I understand, she does not think very highly of him. She dislikes his false humility. Mary has strong opinions on what the character of a gentleman should be."

Darcy's brows rose. "Indeed? I cannot help but agree with her. I had no idea she was so insightful."

Elizabeth chuckled ruefully. "I did not, either. She has been a constant surprise here lately."

At this point, the set ended and Darcy escorted her to the side of the room. Bingley, Jane, Madison, and Charlotte joined them.

"Miss Elizabeth! I did not have opportunity earlier to ask you to dance." Bingley grinned. "May I have your next set?"

Elizabeth laughed. "You may. I thank you for asking."

"May I have your third, then?" Madison bowed. "Miss Lucas assures me that you will not mind my poor dancing skills."

"Mr. Madison. I never said you were a poor dancer." Charlotte put her free hand on her hip as she spoke but never removed the one that held his arm from its spot.

Madison lifted her hand and kissed it. "Of course not, my dear." He winked at her and smiled when she blushed.

"Oh, you." She rolled her eyes and then turned to her friend. "He is an excellent dancer, Lizzy. You will not regret a set with him."

Elizabeth grinned at the banter between her friend and Darcy's. "I will be happy to dance with you for the third set, since Charlotte assures me that I am in no danger from you."

"Excellent." Madison lifted his chin. "I must now find a partner for the second set." He paused. "Aha! Miss Bennet, are you engaged for the next?"

"I am not, sir."

"Then, will you accept me as your partner?"

Jane chuckled. "I will. Thank you."

The first notes of the next dance floated toward them, and they all made their way back to the floor. Darcy hung back, choosing to observe Collins and his movements. He could see the clergyman turning his eyes frequently in Elizabeth's direction. Without letting the other man know he was being watched, Darcy kept him in his sights all night. In the end, his vigilance was not needed.

Chapter 15

Mr. Collins was frustrated. He had been unable to get close enough to Elizabeth to ask her to dance. It seemed as though every gentleman in attendance got to her before he could. *Why did I not ask her before the ball?* he wondered. *Next time I will know better.*

Not only could he not get close enough to obtain her hand for a set, when supper came, she was surrounded by people, sometimes two deep. Jane Bennet, Charlotte Lucas, and even Mrs. Hurst, along with all the gentlemen from Netherfield and two or three of the men of the neighborhood remained close by her side. He decided to try after the meal. The food smelled very good and his stomach had begun to grumble. He parked himself at a table with an empty seat and began to help himself to the delicacies laid out in serving dishes and on platters all down the center of the table at which he sat.

After a while and three helpings of the boiled potatoes from the bowl directly in front of him, Collins heard the orchestra begin to tune their instruments up. He swiftly rose, wiping his mouth with his napkin, and turned. He stopped dead, his jaw dropping open, to see the table where Elizabeth had been sitting completely empty. He searched the now nearly empty room but could not find her. *Oh, no,* he thought. *Where could she be?*

He scurried from the dining room to the

ballroom and began to make his way around the perimeter of the dance floor. His eyes grew wide when he saw his prey walking in the same direction a few feet ahead of him. He rushed toward her, in his haste forgetting his carefully laid out plan. The only thing in his mind at that moment was to grab her and compromise her.

Upon reaching the young lady, he snatched her arm just above the elbow and spun her around, wrapping her tightly in his arms. His momentum pushed him forward and the lady staggered backward. Her heel caught in her hem, which was just a bit longer than it should have been for a ball gown, and she fell, Collins falling with her. They landed in an undignified heap with Collins on top.

Once his breath returned after his fall, Collins felt triumph fill him. "Now, Miss Elizabeth, you will have to marry me. Your Mr. Darcy will not want you now, not after ..." His voice trailed off as he looked into the young lady's face and realized that she was not, in fact, Elizabeth Bennet. His eyes rounded and his lips flapped as he stared at Miss Susanna Long. Suddenly, hands lifted him off the young lady.

"See here, sir! You have compromised my niece! If dueling were not illegal, I would see you on the field of honor right this minute."

"I, I, I did not mean to do it, I swear! Please, I have never held a weapon in my life!" Collins sobbed, holding his hands up in supplication.

"He will do the honorable thing, will he not, Husband? He is a clergyman. Are they not held up as an example of gentlemanly behavior?"

Collins looked toward the young lady, who was being helped up by an older woman he assumed to be his accoster's wife. "I cannot marry her! I have to marry –"

"Now see here!" The gentleman, who Collins now realized must be Mr. Long, drew close, to within inches of his nose. "I have connections, highly placed connections, in the church. If you do not behave honorably, I will go to town in the morning and visit the bishop myself. I will make certain that you are disciplined and refused any further livings."

Collins swallowed. *What am I to do?* he thought. *If he goes to the bishop, I will forever be left with a black mark against me and no hope of advancement. But ... Lady Catherine! She will be exceedingly unhappy with me for failing in my assignment. Will she also be so if the church disciplines me?"* He swallowed again, his eyes darting back and forth, searching for an escape.

"Well, sir?" Mr. Long growled the question.

Collins stammered for a few more minutes, but then noticed the circle of faces that surrounded them. None of them appeared pleased. He became afraid for his well-being. Suddenly, his choice became clear. His shoulders drooped.

"I will marry her."

At the back of the crowd surrounding the Longs and Mr. Collins, Darcy and Elizabeth stood watching the situation play out. Elizabeth held a hand to her mouth, her eyes wide. She looked up at her betrothed.

"He was going to do that to me; that was his plan."

Darcy nodded and squeezed the hand that rested on his arm. When she tightened her grip in return, he entwined their fingers. "I would never have let that happen. Even if I had not been near you, Bingley, Hurst, or Madison would have been. We would have prevented it."

"But, what if he had succeeded? Would you have rejected me for it?" Elizabeth stared up at him.

"No," Darcy declared. "I would never reject you. I could not. I love you to the depth of my being; you are stuck with me for the rest of your life."

Elizabeth chuckled even as her eyes filled with tears. "You are the best man I know. Have I ever told you that?"

"No, you have not." Darcy lifted a hand to caress her cheek. "Am I?"

"You are."

His eyes drifted to her lips. "I would love to kiss you right now."

"I would love it if you did." Her eyes lit with

mischief even as her lips lifted in a smile.

He swallowed, looking around as the crowd dispersed and Mr. Collins and the Longs exited through a side door. "It seems the time has passed for such things. I can no longer hide behind a bunch of people to do it."

"Not that it stopped you before." Elizabeth winked.

Darcy shook his head. He lifted her hand to kiss. "Behave yourself."

"Must I?" She pouted.

He rolled his eyes. "Yes, my enchanting love, you must." He leaned down to whisper into her ear. "At least until we are wed."

"Mr. Darcy!" Elizabeth pretended affront, but her grin gave away her lack of offense.

"Come, my dear. The orchestra has begun another tune. Will you dance with me again?"

"Happily. Lead on!" She giggled as Darcy turned them around and led the way to join the set.

Later, after the ball was over and the carriages were being brought around, Darcy and his betrothed stood near a window in the drawing room, looking out over the driveway. He was startled out of his pleasant contemplations of their last dance by the sound of Lydia's voice behind them.

"I had hoped Mr. Wickham would be here. He is so handsome! Even though Papa said we were not to have the officers at Longbourn, I was hoping he would ask me to dance."

Kitty replied, "I had almost forgotten about him! He would have been an excellent dancer, I am sure. Do you know why he missed the ball?"

"Something about an assignment in London, or so Mr. Denny said."

"What a shame his duties called him away."

Darcy snorted. When Elizabeth looked up at him with a giggle and a smirk, he looked down into her fine eyes, leaned closer and said, "What a blessing that was! I had enough to worry about with keeping you safe." His heart skipped a beat when he noted the adoring look she gave him.

"I cannot help but agree."

Half an hour later, the Bennet carriage pulled up. Mrs. Bennet had somehow finagled things so that her family was the last to leave. Darcy did not mind in the least. It gave him more time with his beloved.

Elizabeth turned to him after he helped her into her coat. "Will I see you later?"

He took her hands in his. "You will, though I do not know when. It might be dinner before I can get away. Do not let my absence keep you from doing what you wish. I will find you wherever you are."

Darcy saw the frown that she was quick to hide.

"Very well. I will stay near Longbourn,

though, perhaps walking in the gardens if it is not too cold."

He grinned. "I cannot see it being too cold for you, my dear." He lifted both of her hands and kissed the fingers. Then, he took her gloves from her, put them on her hands, and tucked one under his elbow. He escorted her to the carriage, handing her up himself.

"I will be thinking of you the entire time we are apart. I love you." He felt her shiver as he whispered the words into her ear. He knew she felt the same when she squeezed his hand before letting go to settle in between Jane and Mary.

~~~***~~~

Mr. Collins paced back and forth in his room. On the table near the window sat his unfinished letter to his patroness. He had begun writing it as soon as he had returned from the ball. He could only get so far, however, before the import of what he had to report made him quiver in fear of the consequences. He stopped in front of the table and looked at the paper and quill. He groaned.

"She is going to be furious," he said to himself. He shook his head and turned to pace once more to the other side of the room. "How can I word this so it is not as offensive?" He thought a bit longer, his steps taking him back in the direction he had come from.

"It is no use!" He stopped and threw his

hands up. "I would be much better to simply say it. I will flatter and exalt her, but lying would be impossible. Not to mention unwise."

With a huff, Collins strode back to the table, seated himself, and finished the missive. He read it over once more, then sanded it, folded and sealed it, and wrote the direction on the outside.

"There," he said. "It is what it is." He slumped, resting his elbow on the table and his head in his hand. "I have failed to properly complete the assignment Lady Catherine gave me. It is inexcusable. She will make my life miserable." He thought about his betrothed and how her uncle had said he had connections in the church. "Perhaps Mr. Long will use his influence to obtain a living elsewhere for me and I can install a curate to serve Hunsford in my place." He heaved a sigh of relief at the thought. Then, he got up and took himself off to bed after placing the missive in a prominent spot where he would remember in the morning to send it off.

~~~***~~~

At Rosings the next day, Lady Catherine accepted the express from her butler. She noted the handwriting with satisfaction and ripped it open with eager hands.

"Who is that from?" Anne entered the room, her companion trailing along behind her.

Lady Catherine glanced up. "Mr. Collins. I

gave him an assignment." She finished reading, a scowl overtaking her features. "However, he seems to have failed at it."

"I cannot imagine why you would be surprised at that." Anne settled herself in her favorite chair and adjusted her shawl more tightly around her. "What was his assignment?"

Lady Catherine opened her mouth to answer but paused instead. She glanced briefly at her daughter then looked at the paper in her hand once more. "I sent him to find a wife." She fought the urge to chew her lip. It would not do to give any indication of unease.

Anne laughed. "Then I can surely see why he failed. What sensible woman would have someone so ridiculous?"

"Indeed." Lady Catherine folded the missive up once more, slipping it into the reticule that dangled from her wrist. She fell into thought as her only child began to chatter on about something she had read the night before. An indeterminate amount of time later, Anne's sharp voice startled her from her contemplations.

"Mother! I asked you a question."

The elder lady looked up from the spot on the carpet at which she had been staring unseeingly. "I apologize. I was woolgathering. What did you ask me?"

A deep frown marred Anne's brow. "Pay attention when I am speaking to you," she snapped. "I should not have to repeat myself."

"Of course. I am sorry." Lady Catherine lifted her chin, clenching her jaw as she did so.

"I asked you how the renovation of the dower house was going."

"I do not know. I am uncertain if the steward has begun it." Rosings' mistress gripped a fistful of her skirt. She sniffed, doing her best to appear haughty. "I cannot fathom why you think it so important. Once you and Darcy marry, you will live at Pemberley and I will remain here to run Rosings."

Anne rose, her countenance reddening and her hands forming fists. "I am not going to marry Darcy. I have told you this time and again." She took a step toward her mother. "I thought I made myself clear enough the last time the topic arose. Do I have to repeat myself?"

Lady Catherine involuntarily flinched when Anne stepped toward her. The memory of the last episode was still vivid. She would not have brought the subject up again, but she was desperate to be rid of her only living child's presence in her daily life and marrying her off was the only way she could see it being done. *She* was certainly not going to leave her home of nearly thirty years. It would be Anne who must go. She wished to shout that at the recalcitrant child, but refrained. Instead, she took a deep breath and reiterated her oft-shared reasoning.

"You and your cousin were formed for each other. You both descend from the same noble line. The joining of two such valuable estates will create a massive and powerful dynasty. You will be the matriarch of the wealthiest family in all England. And, it was the deepest wish of both myself and my dearly departed sister, for whom you are named." She lifted her chin, looking down her nose, her brow creased.

Anne rolled her eyes. "I do not care, Mother. How many times do I have to repeat myself? I do not have to marry. I have Rosings. I have no need or desire to move to Derbyshire and suffer through those cold winters. I will marry as I wish and only if I want to. I do not have to do a single thing you tell me I must and you are deluding yourself if you think I do." She took a further step, decreasing the gap between herself and Lady Catherine. "Again I ask, do I have to repeat myself?"

The matron clenched her jaw. Despite how angry it made her, the girl was becoming enraged and the only way to appease her now was to give in.

"No, you do not."

Anne stood within an arm's length of her mother and examined her with narrowed eyes. "I do not know that I believe you." She stepped forward again, closing the gap between her and Lady Catherine. Staring deep into her mother's eyes, she lowered her voice and said, "Do not make me do something you will regret." She turned and began walking toward the door. "I believe I will take my phaeton and ponies out. I will be gone at least an hour."

She paused with her hand on the door latch. Looking back at her mother, she added, "I expect you to host a card party two nights hence. Mr. Bartholomew Radcliff is home from his tour of the kingdom, as I understand it. He is to be invited, along with his parents. You will see to it." Without waiting for a reply, she opened the door and was gone.

Lady Catherine waited stiffly in her seat for a few minutes. When she saw her daughter's carriage roll down the drive with Anne behind the reins, she allowed herself to exhale, falling back into the chair. *I do not care what she says,* she thought. *As a matter of fact, I do not care what my nephew says, either. I am going to see the pair of them wed and her out of my house if it is the last thing I do.*

Further contemplation did nothing to ease her anger. She gritted her teeth. "She thinks she can control me, does she? We shall see about that." She thought a few minutes longer, then rang for the butler.

"You called, madam?"

"I did. I want two footmen to attend me at once."

Mr. Winters bowed. "As you wish."

A quarter hour later, the pair of young men stood before her.

"My daughter has a large tufted wingback chair in her rooms. It is green and has a matching footstool. I want both of those items

186

removed immediately and taken to the attics. You will replace them with the wooden chair and footstool in the corner of the library. I want the task completed in the next half-hour. If she demands them changed back, you will tell her to come to be about it. Do you understand?"

"Yes, ma'am." The footmen replied in unison and, when she dismissed them, hurried off to do as they were told.

Lady Catherine watched them leave and then looked at her butler, who had stood by as she spoke to the others.

"I want word sent to the coachman. Miss de Bourgh is out in her phaeton at the moment. However, when she next asks for it, she is to be told that it is unavailable. He can make up whatever excuse he chooses." She made a motion with her hand. "He can tell her it needs maintenance or something." She paused. "Tell him that she is to be denied the use of any of the equipages on the estate, as well as the horses, for the next month."

"As you wish, madam." The butler bowed.

"Also, send the cook up here. I would have a word with her."

Mr. Winters inclined his head and turned to leave, walking to the door with his usual quiet dignity and exiting the room to do as his mistress bid.

Lady Catherine watched him go. "Threaten me, will she? I think not. I look forward to witnessing her outrage over the next few days. We shall see just who is the mistress of this estate." She chuckled darkly. "Should I order liver and onions every day for the next week, replace her tea with coffee, or both?" She laughed aloud at the thought of vexing her daughter.

Then, she grew quiet as she pulled the missive out of her reticule and read it again. She pondered the options she had for forcing Darcy to marry Anne. After a time, she stood and replaced the letter. She called for Mr. Winters and gave him further instructions, then headed to her study to await her visitor.

Chapter 16

At Longbourn, Elizabeth and her father were elbows deep into greasing the bearings in the gig's wheels. She had not intended to assist this day. She knew Darcy would be coming to visit at some point and she was not certain she wished to see his rejection of her participation in this favorite activity. However, when Mr. Bennet appealed to her duty of obedience as a daughter, she rolled her eyes and accepted his manipulation, hoping very much to have the task completed before her betrothed arrived. The pair had just pressed the last of the small metal balls into the wheel and leaned it up against the axle when a voice from the other side of the equipage made her jump, hitting her head on the bottom edge of the step.

"Ouch!" She rubbed her head with her forearm as she stood up, ignoring her father's chuckle. "Mr. Darcy! I did not expect to see you so early." She felt herself flush and searched around her for a rag with which to wipe her hands.

Darcy grinned. "I finished my tasks early and rushed over here to see you." He walked around the back of the gig, tilting his head to see what they were working on. "Greasing the wheels, I see?"

Elizabeth stammered a reply. "We are. We have just about finished the job."

Her father did not appear to be so embarrassed. His eyes crinkled.

Darcy began removing his coat. "Would you care for some help? I have no experience, but I have watched my coachman perform the job numerous times."

"Feel free." Bennet looked at his daughter. "Lizzy, let the man in there. Stick close, though. We may still need a hand."

"Yes, sir." Elizabeth did as instructed, removing herself to a position behind her father and allowing Darcy to replace her under the curricle. She listened to their conversation, relieved that her betrothed had not given her a look of disdain and was instead getting his own hands dirty.

"Hold it up, just so." Bennet glanced at Darcy's face. "I hope you do not think less of my daughter for being so closely involved in the maintenance of my favorite equipage."

Darcy looked Bennet in the eye. "No, sir, I do not. I wish I had half her bravery, for I have always loved carriages and everything involved in maintaining them, but my parents would not allow me to share in the work. As I indicated before, I have often witnessed my staff performing the tasks but have never attempted to work on one of my own, not even my favorite curricle. I may do so in the future and ignore the consternation of my staff."

Bennet said nothing more as he and his future son completed the installation of the wheel. They stood together once it was firmly attached and examined it carefully.

"That should do it." Bennet extended a hand to Darcy. "Thank you for your assistance. It certainly made the process go faster. My Lizzy is an excellent worker but she is not as strong as a man. It often takes longer to perform these maintenance tasks because of it. She never complains, though. I am inordinately proud of her will and perseverance." He smiled at his favorite daughter.

"Thank you, Papa." Elizabeth blushed but winked and grinned.

Bennet chuckled. He wiped his hands on a rag, which he then tossed to Elizabeth. "Go ahead and clean up. Show your Mr. Darcy where everything is while you are at it. I am quite certain the two of you have things to discuss, so I will leave you to it, but make sure you are clean before your mother stirs herself from her rooms."

"I will, Papa. Thank you." She turned to her betrothed as her father exited the stables. "So, you do not mind that I do such things?"

Darcy shook his head, advancing toward her and taking the rag from her hand. He used it to wipe the grease away from her fingers. "I do not. I was quite truthful when I said I envy your courage." He paused. "Perhaps after we marry and you inherit the gig, we might maintain it together. We can even buy a new one for just that purpose."

"Or," Elizabeth began slowly, "maybe we can buy an older one that needs restored, such as what my father did with this one, and do the work together?"

Darcy smiled. "I like that even better." He leaned down to brush a kiss across her lips. "I would like to hold you, but both my hands and this rag are covered in grease, and if we are to keep your activities from your mother, it would not do to have handprints on the back of your gown."

Elizabeth sighed. "Very true." She looked up at him with adoration in her eyes, making Darcy's chest swell. "Come, then, we shall put things away, wipe the gig down one more time, and clean our hands. Perhaps then we can sneak into the garden and hold each other for a while."

Darcy winked and kissed her again. "Lead on, my love."

~~~***~~~

The next day, the gentlemen of Netherfield went together for an early-morning ride. They began slowly enough, but soon found themselves racing across the fields. Darcy was the winner of the impromptu contest, with Hurst coming in second, followed by Madison, and then Bingley.

"I thought I would never catch up," Bingley complained. "What have you been feeding those horses behind my back?"

The other gentlemen laughed.

"Come now, my friend," Darcy replied. "You know as well as I that you are no horseman. You have improved greatly in the years I have known you, but you were not raised to ride as we were."

"I was not, and I freely admit that. There were carriages aplenty but the animals were in use pulling them." He shook his head. "I am certain that if my father had understood the emphasis placed by gentlemen on riding, he would have made sure I was accomplished in it."

Hurst laughed. "By the time you have made the purchase of an estate, I am certain you will be as good as the rest of us. You are certainly getting a great deal of practice of late."

"Too true, Hurst!" Madison nudged his mare forward as the rest began to walk toward the house. "There is nothing like the country for improving equestrian skills. London and Rotten Row have nothing to it."

"Yes, I agree." Darcy nodded as he looked thoughtfully ahead. "There is hardly enough space to move in the park, even on the row. Out here there is a vast expanse of fields in which to practice."

With that, the gentlemen fell silent. The path soon narrowed and they were forced to go from four abreast to two. Hurst and Madison moved forward and began a conversation. Darcy and Bingley rode behind, far enough to be able to hear the other gentlemen's voices but not their actual words.

Bingley glanced over at his friend. "I should apprise you on the situation with Miss Bennet."

Darcy's head turned sharply toward the other man. "Indeed? Is it favorable?" He turned his attention back to where he was going.

"It is." Bingley sighed, and Darcy could hear the pleased relief in it.

"Do tell."

"While you and Miss Elizabeth were doing whatever it was you were doing in the back of the garden yesterday, I escorted Miss Bennet and her sisters into Meryton. There is a path to a cottage at the edge of the town. Have you seen it?" Bingley looked at his friend.

Darcy nodded. "I believe I have. It is a narrow lane; you can just see the corner of a house at the end of it."

"Yes, that is the one." Bingley steered the horse around a large rock in the path. "As we approached it, she sent her sisters on ahead to their aunt's home. She asked me if I minded if we stopped at the house down the lane for a couple minutes. I did not, and so we walked down the row. It turns out, the woman who lives there is unmarried. She has a child – a little boy of about six years of age. I said nothing until we were back out at the main road, but then I asked her opinions of the lady and of unwed mothers in general. Her reply was everything I hoped it would be."

"She has sympathy for them, then?" Darcy tilted his head as he shot another glance toward Bingley.

"She does. She said they must have been misled about the intentions of the men who got them with child and that she does not agree with the notion so prevalent in society of blaming the female for falling pregnant and allowing the man to go on with his life unscathed." Bingley grinned. "It was exactly what I had hoped to hear from her; expected, even, given what I have learned of her nature."

"Will you propose, then?"

"I will, very soon, though I may wait until after your wedding. I would not like to take away the attention you and Miss Elizabeth deserve on such an auspicious day."

Darcy snorted. "Well, given some of the gossip that is floating around about why a gentleman of my stature would behave so with a lady of hers, I am not certain we need so much attention."

"Is it as bad as that?" Bingley turned his head toward his friend, his brow creased.

Darcy shook his head. "No, it is not." He sighed. "I simply despise being the object of gossip, is all." He waved his hand to the side. "Ignore me. I am marrying a woman I love deeply, one I cannot live without. I will soon be returning to my beloved Pemberley and starting a family of my own. I am incandescently happy and I choose to ignore the few naysayers who have tried to steal my joy."

"That is an excellent attitude to have! I am proud of you. It is not your usual manner, though. How did you come to this conclusion?"

"Elizabeth taught me it. She insists that she will not allow the opinions of those so wholly unconnected to her to taint the happiness she feels, and she has encouraged me to do the same." He shrugged. "I am much more peaceful being happy, so that is what I have decided to do."

"Good for you! She is a wise woman, your Elizabeth."

"That she is." Darcy grinned.

The four riders were approaching the stables at this point. They were arrested by the sight of a fifth, this one approaching from the driveway. Darcy startled as he recognized the gentleman in red.

"That is Fitzwilliam! I wonder what he is doing here?"

"I guess we shall soon see, shall we not?" Madison looked over his shoulder at his friend. Then, he nudged his gelding into a canter.

A few minutes later, Darcy and his friends were greeting his cousin.

"Welcome to Netherfield, Colonel." Bingley bowed. "Come on inside. You must be hungry if you have ridden here all the way from town."

"Thank you, I am." The colonel greeted all

four gentlemen. "I am glad to see you well, Cousin."

Darcy's brows rose. "Why would I not be?"

"How about I share the tale over a meal?" Fitzwilliam glanced around. "What I have to say should stay confidential, I think, or at least kept between the five of us. Your friends can help me keep you safe."

Darcy frowned. "Very well, we can do that." He gestured toward the drive. "Let us follow the rest up."

A quarter hour later, Colonel Fitzwilliam, his cousin, and his cousin's friends were ensconced in Bingley's study. A pair of maids had just left the room after having delivered trays of food and hot tea. The gentlemen gathered around the table to make up plates for themselves before choosing seats in front of the fire and balancing their meals on their laps.

"So," Darcy said to his cousin. "What is it that brings you so unexpectedly from town?"

Richard looked around the room, then rose and locked the door. He came back to his place and settled himself once more, lifting a forkful of meat pie. "Have you seen Lady Catherine lately?"

Darcy's brows rose. He chewed his mouthful of food twice more, then swallowed. "I have. Why?"

"It seems she has hired one of her tenants to drug you, tie you up, and transport you to Rosings."

Darcy's fork fell from his hand, the handle clattering on the edge of the plate. "*What*?"

Richard gave his cousin a pointed look. "You heard me. She wants you kidnapped and brought to her. I am quite certain you can understand why."

"Why on earth would she think to do something like that? I told her I would never marry Anne. I thought she understood me."

Richard shrugged. "All that notwithstanding, that is her plan."

Bingley's head had been swinging between the cousins. "How do you know this?"

"My father has a spy in her house; one of the servants. This person overheard some things and sent the earl an express to warn him."

"A spy?" Darcy shook his head. "I always suspected he had someone watching what was going on there. Well, then, I assume Lord Matlock had something to say about it?"

"He did." Richard spoke around a mouthful of the savory pie. "He went to Rosings and sent me here."

"Good." Madison leaned forward. "We will need to develop a plan to keep Darcy safe. Do you know what drug she has given this tenant?"

The colonel shook his head. "No; our source did not relay that to us. If my father discovers it, he will send someone here to tell us."

"And in the meantime, what? I have someone taste my food before I eat it?" Darcy set his plate on a table an arm's reach from his chair and stood to stride to the fireplace, where he turned around and faced his cousin. "Is she insane? Does this man know the proper amount to give me, or is he going to dose me heavily enough to kill me? All this, and for what reason ... undoubtedly to try to force me to marry her daughter. That is the only possible thing that might induce her to behave in such a manner." He turned around and slammed the side of his fist on the top of the mantelpiece.

Hurst had been watching Darcy closely, but now had a question for the colonel. "Do we know who this tenant is that Lady Catherine has sent?"

"According to our spy, he is a man named Larkin. Matthew Larkin. I think I recall who he is, but I have never dealt with tenant concerns like Darcy has."

Without turning, Darcy confirmed his knowledge of his would-be assailant. "He leases the worst-performing farm in all of Rosings. He is perpetually behind in the rent but only because he is lazy. He does not maintain the ground as he is supposed to and so it does not yield like it should. That plot of land is capable, with proper management, of being one of the best in the area." He fell silent for a long moment. "I have had words with him more than once."

Fitzwilliam sipped some tea, having eaten

his fill in the swift manner of someone used to having only short breaks for meals. When he had swallowed, he stared at the cup for a moment. "Then, he has reason to be resentful of you, which might explain his obedience to Lady Catherine's demands."

Darcy nodded. "Indeed. He likely also wishes to retain his lease. He has been threatened more than once, by my aunt as well as myself, that he will be evicted if he does not catch up on his rent. Combined with his dislike of me, I would imagine the idea of being forgiven the debt would be a strong incentive to completing the assignment."

"True." Madison stood to place his plate on the table where the food was laid out and to choose a biscuit off the tray. He turned back toward the group of men. "So ... a plan. Do you have any ideas, Colonel? How are we to keep Darcy safe and here in Hertfordshire, and prevent a possible poisoning?"

Chapter 17

Fitzwilliam tilted his head. "I have the basics of an idea, but I welcome any input you gentlemen have. I first propose we interview the staff and find out if there have been any strange men hanging about. Darcy, are you able to give us a description of this tenant?"

"I can."

"Excellent." Richard turned to Bingley. "Can you gather your servants together and share the description with them? Ask them if he has been seen and to alert you if he shows up."

"I will do that." Bingley rose to ring the bell and call the housekeeper.

"What if he has already arrived," Hurst asked, "and has somehow swayed one of the maids or footmen, or even the housekeeper, to allow him access to the house or to drug Darcy's food?"

"We will have to trust that everyone is telling the truth but behave with extreme caution." The colonel looked each man in the eye. "My cousin must not be left alone at any time. We cannot be always in the kitchen observing the cook, nor watching every servant all the time. However, if Darcy is never alone we can at least protect him from a kidnap attempt."

"Perhaps the doors to whatever rooms he is in should be locked, as well." Bingley tilted his head. "What do you think, Fitzwilliam?"

The colonel shook his head. "That is an excellent notion, but if we want to catch this person, we must allow him room to come closer than that."

Hurst shifted in his seat, his brow creased. "Maybe I should send Louisa away for a few days. I do not want her in danger."

"I suspect the colonel wishes for the household to function normally," Madison said. "If you suddenly send Mrs. Hurst away, you could tip off the assailant."

"You are correct. I do want everything to appear ordinary. I do not think it will take long for this man to show himself. By the time your wife is ready to leave, we will have him in custody. We will take the utmost care to keep her out of harm's way."

Hurst's lips thinned but he acquiesced. "Very well. If we are not sending her away, I want her kept in the dark about what is going on. I will inform her after the fact."

The gentlemen agreed to say nothing in front of Louisa. They set up a schedule of who would remain with Darcy and when. Finally, having hammered out the details, Bingley went to meet with his staff and the others went to their chambers to change before meeting in the billiards room for a game.

~~~***~~~

At Longbourn later that afternoon, Mrs. Hill entered the drawing room where the ladies of the house were gathered and handed a note to Elizabeth.

"Thank you." Elizabeth smiled at the housekeeper. She turned the note over in her hand, her brow creasing. "It is from Mr. Darcy. I wonder why he wrote."

With a glance at her mother, who had studiously ignored her second daughter for nigh onto a week, Jane moved from near the fire to the settee where her next younger sister sat. "The only way to discover it would be to open it."

"True." Elizabeth hesitated, but then broke the seal and unfolded the page. She skimmed the contents, then moved back up to the top of the letter and read again.

"Well?"

Elizabeth looked up to see three pairs of eyes drilling into her. She wondered if Mary would be doing the same if she were not in the other room, practicing on the pianoforte. "He will not be able to join us for dinner. One of his cousins has suddenly arrived from London. He hopes to be able to visit tomorrow but says that if he cannot, he will send another note."

"Oh." Kitty's brow furrowed. "I wonder why his cousin has come to Hertfordshire."

"I do, as well. He does not say, though." Elizabeth stared at the page and bit her lip. "I do not think I like this. I hope he is not there to represent another branch of the family that does not wish us to marry."

Jane reached over and wrapped her hand

203

around her sister's. "I am certain that is not the reason. I suspect this cousin simply wished to meet you before the wedding."

"Oh, Jane." Elizabeth sighed "You always think the best of everyone." She paused. "I hope you are correct in this instance."

Jane smiled. "Of course I am correct." When Elizabeth snorted, she winked and then smiled bigger. "When am I not?"

Elizabeth laughed. "When, indeed." With a shake of her head, she tucked the missive into her reticule and picked up her sewing. "I shall just finish embroidering the hem of this gown. I will have plenty of time, I think, to also decorate the neckline."

Jane glanced over at her mother, who was chattering with Kitty and Lydia. Then, in a whisper, she brought up a subject that had been avoided for days. "I am sorry Mama is being difficult about preparing for your wedding. Especially since Mr. Collins is not able to marry you now, anyway."

Elizabeth shuddered. "Poor Susannah Long! At least he has returned to his home. I hope that when he does come back, Papa makes him take up residence at the inn instead of here."

"Lizzy! Do not be unkind."

"You cannot tell me, Jane Bennet, that you wish for him to return here. I hate to sound like our mother, but I do not like him and have no desire to see or hear from him again."

"Well, no, I do not want him to return, but

we must always be open to strangers, or even strange people, coming into our home. We might be entertaining angels, you know."

"You sound like Mary." Elizabeth's grumble came with a lower lip that extended in a pout and made Jane giggle. "Oh, very well. I am sorry for being unkind. I still hope Papa refuses him entrance, though, for your sake and that of our sisters. Even though Mr. Collins is marrying, I somehow do not trust him."

"I understand." Jane squeezed the hand she still held. She let go and picked up her own stitching. "We should get busy before Mama demands my attention."

"I am not sorry she is ignoring me and my wedding plans, you know. The entire ceremony and breakfast will be to my taste and not hers, and that is not a bad thing."

Jane smiled. "I know. I just wish she would give you your due. I am shocked that she appears not to care about our status as a family; the neighbors expect dinners and balls and a grand wedding breakfast and that is not what you will have."

Elizabeth shrugged. "It will be well. Darcy does not like to be the center of attention." She glanced over at her mother. "Besides, you never know when she will suddenly remember it and take over. I say we get as much done as possible on our own as quickly as we can."

"I see your point." Jane nodded. "Let us get busy, then."

For the rest of the afternoon and into the evening, they did just that.

~~~***~~~

At Netherfield, the evening was quiet. The gentlemen kept to their plan of not leaving Darcy alone. Wherever he was in a room, there was someone no more than an arm's length away at all times. If Louisa noticed, she said nothing. Eventually, everyone retired, all at the same time, and the house grew quiet. Darcy had explained the situation to his valet, whom he trusted implicitly, and instructed the man to make certain the doors to the hallway were locked and to have a cot brought up to his bedchamber and set up along the wall by the dressing room door so that he could sleep in the room with him.

The following morning, Darcy and his cousin rode out alone for their morning exercise. They had both risen before the rest of the household, in part because it was a habit they had long had and in part because their sleep had not been particularly restful and they saw no point in lying in bed, staring at the canopy above them.

"Bingley told me he called in the staff from the stables last night so they could hear what he had to say. Everyone on the estate is aware to look out for Larkin." Darcy's words to his cousin were quiet as they stood in the barn waiting for their mounts to be brought to them.

Fitzwilliam merely nodded. He was silent for several minutes, his sharp eyes darting back and forth as he listened and watched and assimilated the sounds, looking for anything out of place. "I suspect he will approach a maid before he tries to get a groom to help him. A maid is more easily able to slip a drug into a pot of tea or bowl of soup. He will only involve a groomsman if he cannot get an in with a house servant. Even then, I think he will be more likely to attempt to spook the horse or something." The colonel shrugged. "There is an abundance of ways he could choose to use to get you."

Just then, the first groom brought Apollo out for Darcy, who grasped the animal's bridle. With a nod for the servant, he began to walk the horse toward the door. Fitzwilliam's mare was not far behind; he followed suit, guiding her out the door and into the paddock. They mounted and rode out without incident.

Thirty minutes later, they returned and handed the reins over once again to the staff. They made their way into the house and up to their chambers, agreeing to meet in the breakfast room in thirty minutes. When Darcy walked into his chambers, he was unsurprised to see Bingley waiting for him.

"How was your ride?" Bingley stood as he spoke.

"Uneventful, thankfully. Come." Darcy gestured toward the dressing room. "I will have

Smith set the screen up in front of the tub and we can talk while I bathe."

Bingley followed his friend into the other room. Darcy did exactly as he said he would and within minutes, was behind the screen, undressing. Once the valet had gone out the door, Bingley locked it and moved to a chair near the tightly-closed window. "Mrs. Nichols informed me a little bit ago that a maid had come to her and told her of a man asking at the back door about the guests here."

In the bath, Darcy stopped. "Did she describe him? Was it Larkin?"

"She did," Bingley replied, "and I believe it was. It did not take him long, did it?"

"No, it did not. We need to tell my cousin."

"I have instructed the servant assigned to him to relay the message."

Darcy was silent for a long moment. "Good," he finally said. "We will speak to him anyway. No offense to you or your servants, but I want to know without the shadow of a doubt that he has been informed."

"No offense taken. I assume Fitzwilliam will want to lure this man inside at some point?"

"There is not a doubt in my mind that he will." Darcy quickly finished his bath. "You need to either unlock the door and let Smith back in or come to this side and pour that bucket of water over my head."

"I will let him back in this instant. I have no need of ever again seeing anything as frightening as you without clothing. The last time we went swimming was terrifying enough."

Darcy laughed as Bingley let Smith into the room.

A few minutes later, after Darcy was dressed and shaved, he and Bingley joined the colonel and the rest of the gentlemen in the breakfast room.

"I have encouraged Louisa to take a tray in her chambers this morning." Hurst walked to the sideboard and made up a plate, then gave it to a maid to take to his wife, along with a pot of tea.

Once they all had plates and the servants had been dismissed, the gentlemen, who had seated themselves all at one end of the table, were informed of the latest news by Darcy and Bingley.

Madison whistled. "I should not be, I suppose, but I am astonished at the speed with which this man has begun his task."

"I am, as well, but I am happy he has." Fitzwilliam waved his fork at each of his companions. "We will need to be vigilant today. I spoke to the housekeeper and the maid in question and instructed them to allow the man in and to do as he asks. They are then to give me a signal that the drug has been added to a food item; there is a different signal for each and a set menu for the day. Darcy ..." He turned to his cousin. "You are to pretend to eat or drink whatever I suggest to you. When you are finished, you are to behave as though you are sleepy ... you can yawn or whatever ... and walk to another room, or, if there is a large enough piece of furniture available, you can lie down and we will go. The rest of you will help me apprehend the man."

Madison's brow rose. "How can we be sure he does not see us?"

"When I get the signal, we will leave the room one at a time. I assume Larkin is aware of the number of gentlemen in the house. He will make note of each one and know when my cousin is alone. Then, he will enter the room Darcy is in. We will have walked to other rooms ... I have noticed that most of them can be accessed through doors between the rooms. One never needs to enter the hallway. When we leave, I will go to the nearest room to the right and enter it. Madison, you do the same to the left. Bingley and Hurst, the pair of you can go further down the hall or even toward the back stairs, but find a place where you cannot be seen."

"There is a water closet under the stairs," Bingley said. "One of us can duck in there and the other can go into the parlor across the hall."

"I will take the parlor," Hurst stated. "I dislike that water closet. It is too small."

"Good. That is settled, then." Fitzwilliam looked at his friends one at a time. "Are there any questions?"

Bingley shook his head. "Not from me. I assume Darcy's safety is of uppermost importance?"

"It is. However, I do not wish for you to put yourselves in any more danger than you have to. I have my sword and Darcy has a pistol, I believe?"

His cousin nodded. "I do, but it remains for the moment in my luggage. I will call for Smith to bring it down to me."

"Do that." The colonel looked around at the gentlemen once more. "If that is all, we should break our fasts and get on with our day. I suspect it will not be long before Larkin strikes."

With that, the five of them ate hearty meals and retired to the library to wait.

Chapter 18

An hour later, the gentlemen having just moved to the billiards room for a quick game or two, Mrs. Nichols knocked on the door. She pushed the wooden panel open when bid and entered with a maid trailing behind her. She looked Colonel Fitzwilliam in the eye and nodded once, then directed the maid to set the tray she held on the table near the window.

Once the servants had gone, Fitzwilliam looked toward the door from his position next to the billiard table to make sure it had been pushed to but not closed entirely. Then, he spoke to his cousin.

"You should have some of that tea, Darcy. It will sooth that dry throat you were complaining about during our ride."

"I will take some, as well," Madison said.

Darcy poured two cups of the brew that the housekeeper had prepared. "How kind it was of Mrs. Nichols to take pity on a bunch of bachelors and steep the tea before she brought it to us." He passed one cup to his friend and then pretended to sip the other.

Both gentlemen went through the motions of drinking for several minutes as the five of them chatted together and Bingley and the colonel finished their game. Suddenly, Darcy set down his cup and yawned widely.

"Oh my. I am sorry. I am suddenly very tired."

Fitzwilliam nodded toward the settee near

the fire. "Perhaps you should lie down on the sofa for a while. You said this morning that you did not sleep well. It would not hurt you to nap, you know."

Darcy yawned again. "Maybe I will."

Hurst put his cue stick away and turned toward the door. "I think I will go check on my wife. She was feeling a bit peaky this morning." He bowed to his friends. "I will see you after a bit, Bingley. We can go out for some shooting."

"Oh, yes! We should do that! I will see you in a few minutes at the front door." Bingley watched his brother leave the room, then bowed to the remaining gentlemen. "I should go change. You are welcome to join us, if you wish."

Madison inclined his head. "I have a letter to write before I can play; perhaps tomorrow?"

Bingley agreed and, with another, more shallow bow, exited the room. Madison was right behind him.

"I will leave you for a few minutes, Cousin. I have a gift for you from my father that I left in the other room. I will go retrieve it; that will give you a few minutes to rest before I drag you outside again." Without waiting for a reply, Fitzwilliam darted out of the room and to the right, then into the study. Once there, he crept toward the door that joined the billiards room, tucking himself in behind it, thankful he had earlier left it open just a crack. From his vantage point, he could see Darcy lying on the sofa. It took only a few minutes of watching before he sprang into action.

In the billiards room, Darcy was stretched out, his muscles tight and ready for action. He heard someone enter after his cousin had exited and opened his eyes just a little. Through the small slit, he could see a figure examining the empty cups of tea. He was glad he had thought to pour the drugged beverage into the potted plant near the table. He closed his eyes again as the man moved toward his position. When a hand clamped over his mouth, he sprang up, grabbing the appendage and pushing the body attached to it away. After a brief scuffle, it was all over. Darcy's cousin and friends had done their parts exactly as they had been told to, and between them had overcome Mr. Larkin and bound him hand and foot.

"Bingley." Colonel Fitzwilliam stood, breathing hard after his exertions. He swallowed. "Call for the magistrate, please."

Bingley nodded from his place at Larkin's feet, hands on his hips as he also tried to catch his breath. "I will do that." He moved away to call for the housekeeper.

"He put up quite a fight." Hurst was bent over at the waist, his hands on his knees. He blew out a breath before he straightened. "Good thing there were five of us and only one of him."

Madison chuckled. "Indeed. If we had not

outnumbered him, we would have been in trouble."

"At least he did not pull a weapon from somewhere." Darcy knelt beside the prisoner, who had stopped struggling but glared at him over his shoulder.

"Check his pockets while you are down there," Fitzwilliam said. "And the tops of his boots. He may have one and simply did not have opportunity to retrieve it."

With a nod, Darcy did as he was bid. When Larkin protested at the rough treatment, he was reminded in no uncertain terms that he was not in a position to make demands.

"Get me off the floor, at least." Larkin had turned his head to look over his other shoulder so that he could see the colonel. "I was only doing what Lady Catherine required of me. I do not deserve to be treated like an animal."

Fitzwilliam sneered. "You deserve worse than that. Who knows what the results would have been for Darcy? Kidnapping is a crime, and my aunt should have known that, as should you."

"What I should have known was that it was too easy. The maid went from suspicious to eager to help me in the space of a day, and Mr. Darcy was left alone too quickly." Larkin shook his head. "It is as though you knew I was coming." He looked over his shoulder once more, his eyes forming slits as he looked up at the colonel.

Fitzwilliam shrugged. "We did. And what is more, we took steps to stop you." He looked the other man over from head to toe, pausing for a moment on the bindings that held his hands behind his back. "Looks to me like we succeeded."

"How could you know? I met with Lady Catherine alone."

Fitzwilliam crouched down beside Larkin's head. "We know everything that happens at Rosings." He looked the other man in the eye. "Everything." He stood then and walked away.

Bingley had done as asked and requested that Mrs. Nichols summon the magistrate. When she returned to tell him it was done, she brought two of Netherfield's burliest footmen with her.

"I thought they might be of service to you, sir," she said when he lifted his brows.

"Very good. We certainly can use them." Bingley waved the servants in and dismissed his housekeeper.

Fitzwilliam had the footmen lift the prisoner off the floor and sit him on the settee, then stationed them, one at each end of the piece of furniture, to guard the man.

"We have bound his feet to keep him from escaping. Once the magistrate takes control of him, you will need to remove those bindings, but keep his hands as they are."

"Yes, sir. He won't get away from us." The servants took up their places, giving Larkin dirty looks as they did.

Darcy and his friends returned to the library after this, keeping open the door between it and the billiards room.

"I could use a glass of port." Hurst headed straight for the decanters on the table near the window. "Anyone else?"

The rest of the gentlemen agreed, and soon the five of them were seated and sipping glasses of wine.

"I have not worked that hard at anything in years." Madison laughed. "It was quite invigorating."

"You seem almost gleeful." Darcy shook his head at his friend. "But then, you always were one to enjoy a physical altercation."

Madison grinned and lifted his glass in a mock salute. "Much to my mother's dismay."

His companions joined him in laughter.

"What happens now?" Bingley turned to Darcy and Fitzwilliam, who sat close to each other in the chairs nearest the fireplace. "I mean, clearly this man ..." He waved toward the billiards room. "... will be charged with a crime and tried, and hopefully punished. But, what about Lady Catherine? If she was behind the plot, what can be done about her?"

Darcy lifted and lowered a shoulder. "I do not know that anything can be done legally, or even should be. I will, however, distance myself from her. She clearly cannot be trusted."

"I am sorry. I know how that feels; I would not wish a rift in the family on anyone." Bingley frowned into his glass.

No one knew how to reply to that. Darcy and Hurst gave him sympathetic looks, while Madison and Fitzwilliam appeared confused. They were all distracted by a knock on the hallway door.

"Sir," Mrs. Nichols said when she had been granted entrance. "The magistrate is here." She moved aside and allowed Sir William Lucas to enter. Then, she curtseyed and exited the room, pulling the door shut behind her.

Sir William was greatly surprised at the tale the gentlemen told him. "I have never heard of such goings on around here. Life is generally quiet in this area; nothing more than a few drunken farmers now and again." He slapped his hands on his knees and stood. "I will lock him up in the town jail. The circuit judge is due in Hertford next week; he can be tried then."

The rest of the men stood when Sir William did.

"Will you require assistance in conveying him to Hertford?" Fitzwilliam nodded to his cousin. "I am certain Darcy can hire someone if need be."

"I can lend you some footmen if you require it." Bingley stood.

"Thank you, Mr. Bingley. You, too, Mr. Darcy. I have two men who share the overseeing of prisoners – bumbailiffs, if you will – so at present, I will not require more. However, I may make the request in the future."

"All you need do is ask." Darcy bowed. "I thank you for coming so quickly."

"I will need you to write out a statement. Perhaps you can do that while I ask Mrs. Nichols to send for my men? As a matter of fact, I should probably get one from each of you who was involved."

"Gladly." Darcy made his way to the desk at the end of the room. Pulling out paper, a pen, and ink, he prepared to write, first mending his pen and then choosing a piece of paper. As he worked, the rest of the gentlemen chatted. When he was finished, he handed the sheet to Sir William and Fitzwilliam went to the desk to write out his account.

Before long, everyone had finished and the two men who tended the jail and its prisoners had arrived. Larkin was untied at the feet and led out to the cart the men had brought, and was taken off to the village jail. Sir William shook the hand of each of the gentlemen of Netherfield.

"I will be heading home now. I promised Lady Lucas that I would not be away long."

"Thank you again for coming so quickly," Darcy said. "I apologize for pulling you away from your family."

"Think nothing of it." Sir William smiled broadly. "I was happy to escape the talk of lace for a time."

Darcy and his friends laughed.

"I think I will ride with you," Madison said.

"I promised Charlotte I would visit; I do not wish for her to be concerned at my tardiness."

Hurst chuckled. "You do not mind discussions of female fripperies, I take it?"

Madison grinned. "I do not. I have grown used to them, living with so many females."

"And you plan on adding another to the mix?" Bingley shook his head. "Better you than me, my friend."

All the gentlemen laughed loudly at that. Then, Madison and Sir William bowed again and walked out the door.

"I think I will write to my father and apprise him of the situation." Fitzwilliam bowed and strode back to the desk to complete his task.

"I should go check on Louisa and give her the news. She will be relieved."

"Was she truly ill?" Darcy tilted his head as he asked the question.

Hurst nodded. "She was. Something she ate last night did not agree with her. It was strange ... the dishes were all her favorites." He shrugged. "Perhaps she was overset with nerves or something and this was the result."

"Maybe. Please thank her for her patience today in my stead." Darcy glanced at Bingley. "I am going to Longbourn. I need to see Elizabeth."

"I will accompany you. I long to see Jane." Bingley turned to the footman stationed nearby and gave an order for his carriage. When he turned back to Darcy, he said. "We can travel in comfort. After wrestling with Larkin, I am not in a mood to bounce around in a saddle."

"You would rather bounce around in a carriage." Darcy laughed. "Very well. I will happily ride with you in your equipage and leave Apollo to his stall."

The gentlemen parted ways at that point, and before too many minutes had passed, Darcy and Bingley were descending from the carriage in front of Longbourn.

Upon their arrival, they were greeted at the door by their ladies.

"How good of you to come, Mr. Darcy." Elizabeth smiled teasingly and arched her brow.

Darcy forced himself to keep his hands to himself. Whenever she gave him that particular look, it was all he could do not to take her into his arms and kiss her senseless. However, her sisters were hanging out of the doorway, shamelessly ogling them ... and eavesdropping.

"I could not stay away. After the happenings of the morning, I had to see you." He took her hand and kissed it before tucking it under his arm. "Is there a place we can talk?" He looked at his friend and Jane, who were in a similar position. "You and Miss Bennet, as well, Bingley. You can fill in details I might miss."

Elizabeth's brow rose and she looked at her sister, but then shrugged and said, "Certainly. We can use the back parlor. Mary is done practicing for the day, and we can open the door to Papa's book room and lock the hall-way door. If we explain to him what we are do-ing, he can chaperone from his desk. Kitty and Lydia know not to enter his library without permission and he will not grant it if we ask him not to."

Everyone agreed, and the four of them proceeded to do as Elizabeth had suggested. Within a few minutes, they were ensconced in the parlor and a fire had been lit. They seated themselves in front of it, where Mr. Bennet could see them. Darcy began to speak, relating the events of the morning and what had preceded them, as well as the reasons behind them.

Chapter 19

Elizabeth sat with her hand over her mouth as she listened, her eyes growing wide. When he was finished, she reached for his arm, squeezing it gently. "Are you well? He did not injure you?"

"I am well." Darcy pressed one hand over hers. "Not a drop of the tainted tea touched my lips and I fought back the instant he reached for me. My friends were upon him within moments. He never had the opportunity to do more than approach, really." He glanced at the open door and, reluctantly, withdrew his hand from its place resting on hers.

"I am shocked that such a thing could happen!" Jane's expression was similar to her sister's. She looked at Bingley. "Are you also well? You did not get injured in the struggle did you? You arrived in a carriage instead of on your horse."

"I am well. I was out of breath by the time we had him subdued, and I confess to having used muscles that have not seen use since I wrestled at home the summer between Eton and University." He chuckled. "I admit to nothing more than being a bit tired."

Elizabeth turned from Bingley to her betrothed. "You say Lady Catherine ordered this man to accost you?"

Darcy nodded. "I did. I believe she intended to try to force me to marry her daughter."

"But ..." Jane looked from her sister to Darcy, then to Bingley, and back to Darcy. "You told her you would not. How can she think to make you bend to her will?"

Darcy shrugged. "There is no explanation that will adequately convey my aunt's thinking. It is a mystery to all of us." He turned to Elizabeth. "I will, however, censure her the best I can, which will mean cutting her from my acquaintance." He saw her mouth open and rushed to continue. "I know it is not the ideal situation. You, with your tender heart, will not like this solution. However, Lady Catherine cannot go unpunished. She cannot be allowed to think she can arrange everything in the world to her desires. If she were not a peer, she could be arrested right along with her henchman. I know my uncle will not allow that; we would all be painted with the same brush and face the scorn of the *ton*. This is the only method I know of to bring her to heel, so to speak. She needs the connections to me and my family, and she knows it."

Elizabeth shook her head and looked away for a moment. Bringing her gaze back to her betrothed, she sighed and conceded. "Very well. You are correct; I do not like it, but I see the wisdom of your solution."

"Will the earl censure her, as well?" Bingley's brow creased. "He will not simply allow her to carry on, will he?"

Darcy shook his head. "I do not know exactly what he will do, but he will indeed censure her. Her behavior reflects poorly on him and he hates that." He shrugged. "I am certain we will learn of his decisions very soon. I know for certain that he will not allow her to continue on as she has been, though. Aunt Catherine has always been domineering, but we have spoken, the earl and I, more than once about how we dislike it. I think he has not moved to stop her before now because nothing she has done to this point has been dangerous. This, however, was."

"Well," Elizabeth said, her brow creased. "There is nothing to do for it but hope that whatever he decides upon will be effective in keeping her in check." She paused. "Since there is nothing we can do right now, perhaps we ought to go for a walk. I could certainly use some exercise after such an intense discussion."

Darcy looked out the window. Though the sun was low in the sky, it was not dark, and he knew the temperature would probably not be too cold. "That sounds like a very good idea to me. As long as we are bundled up well, we should be fine for a short stroll around the gardens."

"Oh yes." Elizabeth laughed. "Let us not venture too far. It is too late in the day to wear fine gentlemen like yourselves out, not after you had such a trying morning."

"Lizzy." Jane chided her sister but giggled nonetheless.

The four young people told Mr. Bennet where they were going and then went into the hall and donned their outerwear. They kept to the gardens closest to the house but allowed a bit of separation between them, with Darcy and Elizabeth, who were better walkers, moving ahead and Bingley and Jane falling behind.

Darcy and his betrothed strolled along in a comfortable silence, her hand on his arm and his fingers entwined with hers. They came to a turn in the path and he happened to look back to see the other couple stopped and Bingley down on one knee. He halted and nudged Elizabeth. "Look," he said, and he tilted his head toward his friend.

"Oh!" Elizabeth's free hand came up to cover her mouth but when she looked up at him, Darcy could see tears glistening in her eyes.

"How do you feel about this?" He tilted his head as he watched her.

"I am happy. Beyond happy, in fact. Jane confided in me a few days ago that she loves him. I am delighted to see that her feelings are returned."

Just then, Bingley and Jane walked up to them, smiling from ear to ear.

"Oh, Lizzy, I am so happy!" Jane reached for her sister's hands.

"Congratulations! I am elated on your behalf." Elizabeth pulled Jane into a hug.

While the ladies were embracing and talking excitedly over each other, Darcy laughed and held his hand out to his friend. "Congratulations. You will do very well together, I think."

"Thank you." Bingley watched Jane, his smile never wavering. "I offered for her earlier than I had planned, but ..." He paused and looked back at Darcy. "After what happened this morning and seeing the danger you were in, I realized that life is precious. Anything can happen at any time. I decided not to wait any longer."

"Have you told her about Caroline?"

"I did, as soon as we got outside. Her response was as I expected; she feels sympathy for my sister's plight and has declared that it would not affect Caroline's acceptance into her home in the least."

"Excellent!" Darcy slapped Bingley on the shoulder. "I am happy for you."

Elizabeth and Jane had stopped talking and rejoined the gentlemen.

"I should go speak to Mr. Bennet." Bingley tucked Jane's hand under his elbow again. "We will see you in a few minutes."

"We will be right behind you." Darcy watched the other couple hurry to the house. Then, with a shake of his head and a grin, he offered his arm to Elizabeth and they followed.

~~~***~~~

The following day saw the ladies of Lucas Lodge visiting Longbourn. Mrs. Bennet was full of Jane's wedding, and still neglecting the planning of Elizabeth's. She did not let her guests get a word in edgewise for a full half hour. Finally, though, she wound down.

"My Charlotte has news to share." Lady Lucas turned to her daughter. "Do you not?"

Charlotte blushed. "I do." She looked around at her friends and drew in a deep breath. "I still can hardly believe it is true, but Mr. Madison has proposed and I have accepted."

Elizabeth gasped and then clapped her hands. "Oh, Charlotte! How delightful!"

When the other girls had expressed their congratulations, the talk turned to wedding celebrations.

"I intend to hold a fete for Jane every week between now and the wedding." Mrs. Bennet sighed, turning her gaze upon her eldest and most beautiful child. "To have a daughter so well married, and living so close to me, is a dream of mine come to fruition. They will wed in six weeks, so I have already begun planning. We will host a dinner Thursday of this week. You must come and join us."

"We would be happy to." Lady Lucas smiled and then, noticing Elizabeth out of the corner of her eye, frowned. "Have you not had a party for Miss Lizzy? Is she not marrying in a few days?"

Mrs. Bennet had no response for a long minute. Her mouth opened and closed twice before she finally found words. "She is. Of course we will have a party for her. I will move Jane's to the Tuesday after the wedding. That gives me more time to plan for it. We can have a dinner with dancing for Lizzy this Thursday. Will you be able to attend both?"

Lady Lucas had been silently watching her neighbor with a small crease between her brows. She nodded and confirmed her family's attendance at the pair of events, as well as Elizabeth's wedding celebration. "You are not still angry that Miss Lizzy is marrying Mr. Darcy and not that awful Mr. Collins, are you? Surely you would not hold a grudge against her for so long."

"No! Of course not." Mrs. Bennet lifted her chin. "I am happy Lizzy is marrying so well." She turned to look at her second daughter, a small smile lifting the corners of her lips.

Elizabeth was stunned at the turn of events. She had not expected her mother to ever relent and recognize her upcoming nuptials, but realized that the threat of being the object of gossip was enough for Mrs. Bennet to change her mind, or at least to alter her behavior. Her eyes widened as she looked at Jane and shrugged.

The conversation took a different turn, then, and Elizabeth was given an opportunity to contemplate the possible results of the interaction. Deciding after a few minutes to wait and see how her mother treated her and how much effort she put into the newly-planned dinner, she was able to engage with the Lucas family with almost as much serenity as Jane.

~~~***~~~

The following week was a whirlwind of activity for both Elizabeth and Darcy. He was constantly with her during the day. He made visits with her to the families in the neighborhood, often going along with Mrs. Bennet as she made her rounds. They made several treks to Oakham Mount, and took many strolls through Longbourn's gardens. There was a dinner with dancing at the Goulding residence, and there was Mrs. Bennet's planned evening.

The day after the engagement dinner, Darcy and Elizabeth decided to remain close to the house, and walked no further than the wilderness area at the back of the garden. They made their way in the comfortable silence they were wont to enjoy, but when they reached their destination, he settled her on a bench, seated himself beside her, and made an observation.

"It seemed last evening as though your mother may have forgiven you for your audacity in accepting me."

Elizabeth made a noise and shook her head. "I suppose she has, though she still has not forgiven you for speaking so meanly of her youngest daughters."

A crease developed in Darcy's brow. "Is that why she has fought our betrothal so hard?"

"It is." Elizabeth paused. "I notice you do not deny her allegation."

Darcy shrugged. "I have a distinct memory of telling someone ... either Madison or Bingley ... that I did not feel them to be mature enough to be out in public. Even you have indicated feeling that way." He looked at her.

"I have, and I often do feel that way. I am not upset with you. How could I be when you so charmingly proposed to me despite their behavior?" She looked up at him with her brow arched and her lips pursed.

Darcy took a deep breath. The desire to kiss her, though always present, would forever strike him hard when she looked at him that way. He steeled himself not to give in, and as a result, took a while to reply.

"I will never regret giving in to the impulse of the moment that night. It was the first time I had done such a thing since I was in short pants, but ..." He paused, lifted their joined hands, and kissed her fingers. "That one impulsive moment changed my life forever, and for the better."

~~~***~~~

Darcy's aunt and uncle, the Earl and Countess of Matlock, reached Netherfield in the early afternoon of the day before the wedding. Bingley was eager to host them and the rest of their family; their eldest son, Trevor Fitzwilliam, Viscount Tansley, and his viscountess,

Vanessa, came along, as did both of their daughters, Lady Constance and Lady Susan. Darcy's sister, Georgiana, had travelled to Hertfordshire with them. Colonel Fitzwilliam, the earl's second son, was already in residence, of course. The groom was happy to have the family members that meant the most to him witness the most important day of his life.

Elizabeth was pleased to hear that her betrothed's side of the church would not be as empty as she had feared it would be. When he came for a short visit that evening, she teased him about it.

"So there are people in this world who care enough about you to attend your wedding. Peers, no less." She looked up at him with the arched brow that she knew he loved and pursed of her lips.

Darcy chuckled. "Indeed, there are. Proof positive that Lady Catherine has no idea what she is talking about."

Elizabeth laughed and squeezed his arm. "I am happy they arrived safely. I am disappointed, though, that you did not bring your sister with you to meet me."

"I wanted to, but Georgiana did not wish to intrude, knowing that I would return to Netherfield early instead of dining with you. She says she is content to meet you tomorrow at the breakfast, so I did not push her." He shrugged. "I even tried to persuade her by reminding her that there would be far fewer people here today than there will be tomorrow. She is shy, you know, and does not like crowds. But, she would not be moved and so here I am ... alone." He looked down at her, widening his eyes and forming a pout with his lips.

Elizabeth rolled her eyes. "Silly man." She laughed. "I am happy you came to visit. I worried you would not. It would have been a very long wait to see you again if you had stayed away."

Darcy lifted her hand and kissed it, then intertwined their fingers when he laid it back onto his arm. "I would have gone mad had I not seen you today." He halted his steps, and Elizabeth stopped alongside him. Turning to face her, he lifted his free hand to brush the backs of his fingers down her cheek. "I cannot bear to be parted from you, you know. The closer the wedding comes, the stronger the feeling." He slipped his hand behind her head and drew her closer as he lowered his. "I love you," he whispered just before he pressed his lips to hers for a long and satisfying kiss.

Chapter 20

The day of the wedding finally arrived, much to the relief of both Darcy and Elizabeth. They had survived Mrs. Bennet's sudden interference in the planning of their big day.

Elizabeth pondered that kiss and the conversation that had preceded it as she sat in front of her vanity table. She was dressed only in her chemise, stays, and robe, and Sarah, the maid shared by all the Bennet ladies, was adding the final touches to her hair.

"There you be, miss. All done."

Elizabeth turned her head back and forth as she examined the intricate braids and curls. "It is beautiful. You have outdone yourself." She smiled into the mirror at the blushing servant.

"Thank you, Miss Lizzy." She looked at the small clock that sat on the mantel in Elizabeth's room. "Shall we get you dressed, then?"

"I suppose we should." She stood just as a knock sounded on the door. "Come in," she called.

The door opened and Jane poked her head around it. "I came to help you get ready." She entered and closed the wooden panel behind her. "It will be the last time we will be together this way." She looked down and swallowed. "I did not wish to miss it."

"Oh, Jane." Elizabeth took the two steps forward that allowed her to stand close enough to pull her sister into her arms. "Do not dare cry. It is too close to the time of the ceremony and it would not do for me to arrive at my wedding with a red, swollen face and watery eyes."

Jane laughed. "I suppose it would not. I will endeavor to control myself, then."

Elizabeth giggled and the two fell into paroxysms of mirth. They almost missed another knock on the door. When it opened, Mary stood in the hall, asking to come in.

"Of course you can!" Elizabeth pulled her inside and soon the three girls were indulging in a group hug and more laughter.

Eventually, Jane stepped back. "Time is ticking away. We must get you dressed." She accepted her sister's gown, a lovely lilac-colored silk confection with dark purple flowers and green stems and leaves embroidered on the hem, sleeve edges, and collar, and turned back toward the bride. She and Mary helped Elizabeth into it and buttoned it up the back. On her head they placed her brand-new bonnet with its purple ribbon that matched the flowers on the gown. Then, they turned her toward the mirror.

"Mrs. Darcy." Mary whispered the words as she watched her sister in the reflection from the looking glass.

Elizabeth smiled softly. "Not yet," she replied quietly. "Soon, though."

"Very soon." Jane glanced at the clock. "Come.

Papa will be waiting."

"Mama was ill this morning; she left just before I knocked on your door." Mary picked up Elizabeth's gloves and began to put one on her elder sister's hand.

"She was ill?" Elizabeth's brow creased. "Is it her nerves? She does not expect us to postpone the ceremony, does she?"

"She seemed to be recovered." Mary kept her focus on her task and soon had the second glove on Elizabeth's other hand. "I would not delay if it were me. Get yourself married and away from Mama's anger as fast as possible."

Jane handed her younger sister the bouquet made of roses Darcy had had brought down from Pemberley's conservatory. "I think she is softening toward Mr. Darcy. It was he she was angry with, not Lizzy."

Mary snorted, then blushed. "I am sorry. That was rude." When Elizabeth and Jane assured her all was well, she continued. "Mama has always said Lizzy tries her nerves, and she was more angry than I have ever seen her when Mr. Darcy compromised her. I suspect she was every bit as angry at our sister as she was at him. She wanted to remain here at Longbourn when Papa passes, I think, and Lizzy dashed all her hopes."

"I suppose you may be right." Jane frowned.

"I think she is." Elizabeth arched her brow at her older sister. "I just hope she gets over

239

her anger at him. I do not like rifts in the family, and Darcy is not pleased with her neglect of our wedding plans."

"I am sure she will." Jane brushed her hand down Elizabeth's arm and twitched her skirt into place. "There. You are perfect. One more kiss and hug and we will go downstairs with you."

The girls did just that, and within a few minutes were being greeted by their father.

~~~***~~~

The wedding itself proceeded as all such ceremonies do. Vows were spoken, prayers were prayed, sermons were listened to, and the register was signed. The newly-minted Mr. and Mrs. Darcy exited the door of the church to a shower of rice and seeds and a resounding cheer. Longbourn church was only steps away from the manor, so they walked, moving quickly because the air had turned colder and they were eager to get inside the warm house. They were the first to arrive, and once they had shed their outerwear, they removed to the drawing room, standing in front of the fire and holding hands. Soon, the mistress of the house bustled in and a receiving line was formed.

Once everyone arrived, Darcy and Elizabeth led the way to the dining room, where the table was laid out and a sideboard groaned under the weight of a plethora of dishes. They seated themselves where Mrs. Bennet indicated they should, and plates of food were set before them. They had little opportunity to eat, though, because everyone who had been invited wished for a bit more conversation than was able to be had in the receiving line.

Eventually, once their plates had been mostly cleared, the newly married couple and their guests moved back into the drawing room, where they continued to visit with well-wishers.

"Congratulations, Nephew!" The earl greeted Darcy with a slap on the back. "Will you not introduce me to this beautiful new niece you have given me?"

"Of course I will." Darcy turned toward Elizabeth. "Please meet Mrs. Elizabeth Darcy. Elizabeth, this is my Uncle Henry, Earl of Matlock. Beside him is my Aunt Audra, Countess of Matlock."

Elizabeth curtseyed and smiled. "I am pleased to make your acquaintance. Mr. Darcy has told me much about you."

"All good, I hope?" Lady Matlock smiled and reached for Elizabeth's hand. "He has written to us about you and I feel like I have known you forever. My son Richard seconded Darcy's opinions about you. Welcome to the family, my dear."

"Thank you, my lady. I am happy to have finally become a Darcy. I hope to do my husband and all his family proud."

Darcy smiled at Elizabeth's words. Then, he

became serious and spoke again to his uncle. "Tell us about Lady Catherine."

Lord Matlock sobered immediately. He sighed, but then, with a shake of his head, began to tell his tale. "It seems there has been a struggle between your aunt and cousin over who is in charge of Rosings. Anne has been exerting herself, often in an unpleasant manner, and Lady Catherine, rather than confront her daughter, has been attempting to slyly gain her own desires. She did send Larkin to Hertfordshire to retrieve you. She wanted Anne to marry you because then you would take your wife to Derbyshire and Catherine would once again be the unchallenged mistress of Rosings. As long as Anne remains at home, or marries where she would live near to it, she would 'forever have her nose in Rosings' business', as your aunt put it. She appeared unconcerned with any repercussions to you as far as being drugged goes."

"She shrugged when he brought up your concerns!" Lady Matlock shook her head. "She assumed this Larkin fellow had used the substance before and knew what he was about. I told her it was the height of stupidity to make such an assumption."

"I am confused." Elizabeth's brow creased as she looked from the earl to her new husband. "I am unfamiliar with the law, but as I understand it, a couple cannot get married without having banns read or purchasing a license. How did she expect you to do this when you had already purchased one?"

"That is a good question, my love." Darcy looked at his uncle. "And how did she think to gain my assent? I told her in no uncertain terms that I would not marry my cousin. There are no circumstances in which I could have been persuaded to. If I were drugged, I could not marry, anyway. The clergyman could not in good conscience perform a wedding when one of the couple was clearly not of a sound mind, and if I had been drugged, I would not have been. Nor will he marry two people when one is bound hand and foot, which is what Lady Catherine would have had to do to get me to the altar."

The earl shook his head. "I believe she does understand how the marriage process works. This was the desperate act of a desperate woman who saw her one chance of getting what she wanted slipping through her fingers. Rather than teach her daughter how to behave when Anne was a child, my sister indulged her. Now the girl is an adult and wants her own way. Catherine is unwilling to give it to her, and instead of setting the rules and enforcing them, she has tried to impose her own will on the situation."

Darcy's brow creased. "Has she any consequences?"

The earl nodded. "She does. She is to have no contact with you until you agree, and I am taking over the reviewing of her accounts. She protested that you have done it for the last five years and your father did it for fifteen before that, but I was firm with her. Her expenditures are to be strictly monitored in the future so that she cannot attempt anything else that will open us to danger or scandal. If she continues as she has been, I will restrict her access to her funds.

"As for Anne, I was surprised at her rebelliousness. I witnessed some of this struggle for power that I mentioned, and it is no wonder my sister has become so thoughtless. However, it cannot remain that way. Anne has another year before she inherits. I have told her I want her to marry, and Audra offered to sponsor her for the coming season. However, there is a gentleman in the neighborhood that Anne wishes to wed, so I will endeavor to make that happen for her. It seems he has been coming to visit often. I suspect my sister knew about their little romance, and chose to ignore it."

Darcy shook his head, his lip curling. "I can promise you that any acceptance of attentions from Lady Catherine will only come after receipt of an abject apology and a period of improved behavior.

"I am not as surprised at Anne's conduct as you seem to be. Even when we were children, she demonstrated a desire to get her own way. She was not pleasant to her playmates, though she always gave the appearance of an angel to adults." He rolled his eyes. "I do not see us spending much time with her even if she does marry, though that is not a result of the attack on me."

"I wish one of you had said something when you were younger," Lady Matlock cried. "We could have intervened earlier and, perhaps, this situation would not have arisen."

"Would you have listened?" Darcy looked at the countess with his eyebrows raised. "You always praised Anne and scolded us boys. You could never believe that she would instigate anything."

Lady Matlock flushed and looked away. "Perhaps you are right." She looked Darcy in the eye. "I am sorry I made you feel that you could not come to me and be believed. Please forgive me."

"I do forgive you. It is water under the bridge now. I am certain her behavior is too ingrained at this point to change it. The best we can hope for is that the influence of a husband will inspire her to behave differently." He looked down at Elizabeth, who barely came to his shoulder. "I can attest to the power of love giving one a desire to improve oneself."

Elizabeth's eyes twinkled at him as a grin spread over her features. "Indeed." She squeezed his arm close to her side.

Lord Matlock cleared his throat. "Well, then. I suspect losing your good opinion will

be a sufficient deterrent to my sister. We ..."
He used his hand to indicate himself and the
countess. "... spoke with Anne and stressed to
her the impropriety of her behavior. I am not
certain she heard above half what we said.
But, we will return to Rosings on the morrow
and contact this young man and his family. I
hope to have your cousin married before
spring and your aunt reined in, as well." He
shrugged. "We shall see what happens."

Darcy nodded. "Thank you. That is all we
can expect. I do not see Lady Catherine bowing to your edicts, but as you said, we shall
see. I wish you all the best in the endeavor."

The earl cleared his throat. With a glance
behind Darcy, he replied, "I will stop monopo-
lizing your attention for the time being." He
nodded to a spot just beyond his nephew's
shoulder. "I see your sister hovering; I know
she would not wish to interrupt a conversation. She has been eager to meet your bride."

"We could hardly keep her still all the way
here from Netherfield." Lady Matlock chuckled. "I feared she would bounce out of the carriage window."

Darcy grinned as Elizabeth laughed. They
said goodbye to the older couple and then
turned to see Georgiana light up and hurry
over. She threw her arms around him and
hugged him tightly. He wrapped his around
her shoulders and kissed the top of her head.

"Are you happy, Sprite? You act as though

you have not seen me in days instead of a couple of hours."

"I am!" Georgiana pulled back and looked into his eyes. "I am so happy for you. Congratulations!" She looked down as she loosened her hold on him. "Will you introduce me to my new sister?"

"Of course I will!" Darcy took Elizabeth's hand once more and placed it on his forearm. "Sister, please meet Mrs. Elizabeth Darcy." He looked into his wife's eyes and felt himself falling into them again. He did not, however, forget his duty. "My love, please meet my sister, Miss Georgiana Darcy."

The ladies bowed to each other, rising from their curtseys with matching smiles.

"I am pleased to make your acquaintance, Miss Darcy." Elizabeth shot a mischievous look at her new husband. "Your brother has told me many things about you."

Georgiana shot her brother a look, her eyes narrowing. "All good, I hope."

"Oh, very good, I assure you." Darcy darted a couple wide-eyed glances from his wife to his sister and back. When Elizabeth laughed merrily and his sister followed suit, he relaxed, twisting his neck against the sudden tightness of his cravat.

"I think we frightened him." The new Mrs. Darcy winked at Georgiana.

"I suspect we did. I confess I enjoyed the experience. It is not often I am able to best my

247

brother in anything." Georgiana grinned.

Darcy said nothing. He rolled his eyes, but his joy at seeing his shy little sister drawn out of her shell by the most important woman in his life was immeasurable. He decided to remain silent and simply soak in the conversation.

"I must admit that I am happy to add you to the number of my sisters. Have they introduced you to the neighbors?"

"They have! Miss Bennet and Miss Mary have gone out of their way to make me feel welcome. They introduced me to your Aunt Gardiner. She is so warm and friendly! Brother told me he liked her and your uncle, so I thought I probably would, as well, and I do."

Elizabeth smiled up at her husband for a moment before she replied. "I am happy to hear it! I never had the chance to ask him yesterday what he thought. I was a bit anxious about the introduction, because my uncle is in trade, but they did seem to get along quite well."

Darcy lifted her hand and kissed it. "Your uncle is famous in certain circles. It is a boon to my standing to be able to claim the connection." He chuckled when she rolled her eyes. "I hate to pull you away from each other when you are forming such a bond, but if we are to reach town before dark, we must leave in just a few minutes."

Though they expressed disappointment, both his sister and his wife accepted his words. They hugged and kissed and promised to spend hours together after the wedding trip. Then, he and Elizabeth made their rounds, saying farewell to the family, friends, and neighbors that were gathered. Within a quarter hour, the couple was in their carriage and on their way to spend the night at Darcy House in London. They would make their way to their estate in Scotland the next morning.

Epilogue

Darcy House

London

A month later, Darcy and Elizabeth were back in town and the knocker was on the door. The earl and countess hosted a ball to introduce Elizabeth to their society the day after their nephew and his wife returned.

The day following the ball, the newlyweds were inundated with callers, as had been expected. Though Elizabeth was largely unimpressed with the members of high society she was meeting, they were clearly equally unimpressed with her, and she did not repine the loss of their good opinions. She did, however, find two or three other young wives she felt she could be friends with. It was a relief, for she was a lady who enjoyed the society of others and she had not been looking forward to pretending enjoyment at events where she had no one to confide in.

After the day of visits, Elizabeth joined her husband in his study, where he was enjoying a glass of port with his cousin.

"Good afternoon, Mrs. Darcy." Richard bowed to her. "How are you enjoying being tied to my stuffy cousin?"

Elizabeth laughed. "I like it very much." She raised a brow. "Should I not? After all, he is the exact gentleman to bring out my best qualities."

Fitzwilliam shook his head. "I can see that you do, indeed, suit him well." He seated himself and picked up his glass. "I am very happy to hear it." He lifted the drink in salute. "To Mr. and Mrs. Darcy. May your love always blind you to each other's faults."

"Hear, hear!" Darcy lifted his glass, as well. He took a swallow and then chuckled. "You need a wife, Richard, to soften your rough edges."

The colonel smirked. "Indeed." He turned to Elizabeth. "How is your family? Have you heard from them?"

"I have." Elizabeth bit her lip for a moment and tilted her head. "My sister Jane marries in a fortnight. We will, of course, attend. We will be staying at Netherfield, as I understand it. Will we not, Husband?" She arched her brow as she turned her attention to her spouse.

Darcy felt his heart rate increase at her impertinent look. He swallowed but gathered his wits so he could form a reply. "We will. Bingley has more room and very little family. He will not mind us occupying a chamber and will appreciate the support."

"Excellent!" Fitzwilliam smiled and then looked back at Elizabeth. "And, the rest of your family?"

"I have only heard from Mary. My mother seems to be so wholly focused on Jane's wedding that she does not have time to write, and my father is a dilatory correspondent at best. My two youngest sisters simply asked Mary and Jane to add notes to their letters."

"I see." Fitzwilliam hesitated. "How is Miss Mary?"

A look of dawning understanding crossed Elizabeth's features. "She is very well. She is looking forward to coming to London to stay with the Gardiners for a few weeks following the wedding."

Darcy almost laughed at the relief that spread across his cousin's mien.

"I see." Fitzwilliam looked into his glass. "That is good." He paused again. "Has she found any beaus in the last few weeks?"

Elizabeth's lips twitched, but she answered his question with solemnity. "She has not mentioned any. There are few gentlemen of marriageable age in the area around Meryton. I hope she will meet someone when she is in town. She deserves a good husband who will love her above all others." She looked at Darcy and smiled. "As I have done."

Darcy smiled back as he gazed into her eyes. The sound of the colonel clearing his throat brought him out of his haze, and he turned his attention toward his cousin.

"Have you heard anything more about Wickham?" He turned to his wife. "I had asked Richard before our wedding to look into a post for him that was far from society."

The colonel nodded. "I do have news. As you know, Wickham was in the militia and I am in the regulars, but I do have connections in that branch of the army. I found him a position in a unit in Northumbria, serving under a colonel who is known to be strict. It seems our old friend did not like the discipline required and disappeared. He had convinced the daughter of a local estate owner to elope with him. They married in Gretna Green and came back to her parents' home. The family was unhappy but agreed to the union, as long as they had a settlement in place." Fitzwilliam chuckled. "It seems that the father had it written into the settlement that both the dowry and the inheritance ... she is an heiress ... are to remain in a trust of some sort, controlled, as I understand it, by her father for now and a set of trustees after his death. Wickham gets a yearly stipend and that is it."

Darcy laughed. "I could not have arranged it better! Good for the father!"

The colonel laughed. "Oh, there is more. My contact tells me that the young lady has turned into quite the shrew. She keeps him tightly under her thumb, and Wickham cannot make a move without her permission. Word has it, he is miserable and spends most of his evenings in a drunken stupor."

Darcy laughed at that until tears ran down his face. "It could not have happened to a more deserving person," he finally said. "Would that

I could witness this with my own eyes."

The laughter continued for a few more minutes before they trio calmed.

Fitzwilliam took a sip of his drink. "Has my father informed you about our aunt and cousin in Kent?"

"He mentioned that he had brokered a marriage for Anne."

The colonel nodded. "Yes, she is now engaged to the son of her neighbor. She is happy, my mother tells me, and is planning her own wedding. She will not allow Aunt Catherine to have any say at all. It seems her intended takes no steps to mediate. He allows Anne to do and say what she will."

Darcy's brow creased. "That does not bode well for him."

"Oh?" One of Elizabeth's brows rose. "Are you saying you do not give me my way whenever I ask?"

Darcy felt himself flush. "I did not say that, my love." He grew hotter when his cousin laughed at him.

"I suppose I will discover the truth of such things if I ever marry." Richard hid his smirk behind his glass.

Darcy scowled. "I suppose you will."

Elizabeth winked at her husband but asked a question of the colonel. "How are things with Lady Catherine?"

"As Father tells it, she is furious with him

for following through with his censure. She constantly writes to him to ask for more funds, insisting that her allowance is inadequate. He is so tired of hearing her complaints that he has instructed his butler to forward all correspondence received from Rosings to his solicitor, and that gentleman has begun sending her a standard reply, stating that she has received her funds for the quarter and that there are no more available."

Darcy shook his head. "I am glad he took over that responsibility. Elizabeth still urges me to reconcile, but it will be a long time before it happens. Hearing what you have just related tells me that I am correct to wait. I meant it when I said I needed to receive an apology and see improvement in her behavior before I can accept her back into my circle."

"No one blames you for that." Fitzwilliam's countenance grew somber. "I think we have all tired of her nonsense."

The three were quiet for a while as they pondered Lady Catherine. Finally, Darcy checked his watch and noted the time. "We should dress for dinner. Will you join us?"

The colonel's face brightened. "I will. Why else would I come here but for a dinner invitation?"

"I do not know. Perhaps to drink more of my port?" Darcy raised a brow as he looked at his cousin with his lips turned down. He could not maintain the look, though, and soon was grinning. He stood, helped Elizabeth up, and slapped Fitzwilliam on the shoulder when the colonel rose. "Come; Baxter will set you up in your usual room and assign you a man for the evening." With that, he held his arm out for his wife to hold and led her out of the room and up the stairs.

~~~***~~~

Pemberley, Derbyshire

September 1812

"My love, you have a letter here from your father." Darcy handed his wife the missive, leaning down to kiss her as he did so.

Elizabeth returned his kiss and then moved her feet off the settee so he could sit close to her. "Mama was due to deliver last week. I wonder if this is their announcement." She snapped the seal, unfolded the note, and read it through.

"Oh," she cried, her hand going to her mouth. "It is a boy! They had a boy!" She started to cry and Darcy pulled her into his arms.

"So the entailment is at an end." He kissed her hair as her sobs began to subside. "If this had only happened years ago, how different your life might have been." He pulled a handkerchief out of his pocket and pressed it into her hand.

"I know. That was all I could think of ... it is such a relief to know that things will not end for the Bennet family as we all grew up thinking it would."

"You were surprised when you received the news that your mother was increasing. You must have gotten your hopes up quite high."

Elizabeth sniffed as she wiped her nose. "I suppose I did without realizing it." She settled deeper into his arms and picked up the letter again. "I am sure my mother is ecstatic. As soon as she is churched, she will have that child carted all over Meryton, showing him off."

Darcy chuckled. "Can you blame her?"

She shook her head. "No, not really." She looked up at him. "Our children will have an uncle close in age to them. How strange that will be."

Darcy hugged her. "Indeed." He peeked over her shoulder. "Did your father tell you what they have named him?"

"Oh!" Elizabeth read it through again. "Here it is. Albert Thomas George Bennet. He is named after his father and his grandfathers."

"Well, we must send a gift for Master Albert to welcome him to the family." He squeezed her shoulder.

"We should."

Elizabeth's murmured response made Darcy tilt his head.

"What else does the letter say?"

She looked up. "Mary and Richard were visiting when Mama went into labor. Papa says the colonel kept him very good company while they waited and that my sister was invaluable in assisting Mama, as was Jane. Bingley was a bundle of nerves, apparently."

"I think your father intimidates Bingley. He was probably afraid of becoming the butt of one of his jokes."

Elizabeth shook her head. "Probably, but Papa is harmless. I hope Bingley learns this sooner rather than later." She looked up at Darcy and pursed her lips, asking for a kiss.

Darcy happily obliged her and several long minutes were lost as they indulged in a favorite pastime. When he caught his breath afterward, he had another question.

"Do you think your mother will forgive me now for disparaging Kitty and Lydia?"

Elizabeth laughed. "Oh, I am sure she will. Her focus now will be on little Albert. Plus, it was because of her connection to you that her middle daughter married. She will probably want us to still take one or both of the girls this season, I am sure, but the pressure has been removed. She no longer has to worry about the hedgerows, so she may decide she needs Kitty and Lydia to assist her for a while. It has been something like eighteen years since she had a baby in the house, after all." She looked at his pile of correspondence, which he had dropped in his lap when he pulled her close. "Have you received any good letters?"

Surprised, Darcy removed his arm from around her shoulders and picked up his missives. "Yes, as a matter of fact, I do. This one is from Rosings but is in my uncle's handwriting." He broke the seal and read it through.

"What does it say?" Elizabeth tilted her head as she watched him read.

"You remember how Lady Catherine has been making your cousin's life miserable?"

Elizabeth nodded slowly. "I do."

"Well, it seems she will not be anymore." He lowered the page to his lap. "It appears your cousin received word of his 'disinheritance', if you will. Mrs. Collins sent a note to Rosings two days ago saying that her husband had not taken the news well. She sent him out to work in the gardens in the hopes that such activity would calm him."

"And?"

Darcy took a deep breath. "It seems he decided to check his hives. He was attacked by a swarm of bees and passed away from the attack."

Elizabeth's eyes had grown wide. "Oh, my." She put her hand to her mouth as she stared at him for a long moment. "This is horrible to say, but Susannah must be relieved. I know she was unhappy being married to him. Jane told me her beau was distraught the day Collins married her and that he has not paid attention to any other lady since then. If they are both still interested, they will be free to marry once her mourning is over."

"If he is smart, he will stake his claim as soon as possible. To be honest, since she will be losing her home now, no one would look askance at her for marrying soon. Is she with child, do you think?"

Elizabeth shrugged. "I do not believe so. I have not heard anything, anyway." She shrugged. "I guess we will find out sooner or later." She looked up at Darcy. "Do you ever regret compromising me?"

Darcy shook his head. "Never. I remember telling you that I do not regret that impulsive moment because it changed my life for the better. I did not realize when I said it how true it was." He bent his head and kissed her again, not stopping until some indeterminate time later, when his sister walked in on them and gasped.

~~~***~~~

In the end, Mrs. Bennet did get over her dislike of Darcy. She even gave up her never-ending criticism of her second daughter. As predicted, her son was more important than anything else that might have once held her attention.

~~~***~~~

Susannah Long Collins did marry her former beau. After her husband's funeral, she returned to her parents' home. John Goulding called on her that very day and was a constant visitor. There was no question of a child from her first husband, as she had loathed him from the beginning and never once allowed him into her bed. Susannah and John eloped a month after her return and lived a long and happy life together, welcoming six children into the world.

~~~***~~~

Jane and Bingley eventually gave up Netherfield and purchased an estate just thirty miles from Pemberley. The two couples were in frequent company with each other and their sister Mary, who, with her husband, had taken up residence at the dower house at Matlock upon his retirement from the army.

~~~***~~~

After Darcy's marriage, Georgiana happily lived full-time with him and her new sister, and between them and her companion, Mrs. Annesley, grew and matured into a confident but pleasant young lady. She came out when she was eighteen and was declared a diamond of the first water by the leaders of the *ton*. She fell in love in her third season with a gentleman from Lincolnshire named Stephen Lethbridge. The couple raised five children to adulthood and lived a long and happy life.

~~~***~~~

As he had promised, Darcy purchased an elderly curricle and helped his wife to restore it. Elizabeth taught him everything she knew, and they passed many a happy hour working on the equipage. When Mr. Bennet passed and his gig came to Pemberley, Darcy had a building erected specifically for the pair of antique carriages. He and his wife could often be found driving around in one or the other of them.

~~~***~~~

Elizabeth bore Darcy eight children: four boys and four girls. Eventually, her husband turned over the reins of the Pemberley estates to his eldest son, Bennet. Darcy and his Elizabeth were married for seventy years and died within hours of each other one cold winter morning in 1881.

The End

Before you go ...

If you enjoyed this book, please consider leaving a review at the store where you purchased it.

Also, consider joining my mailing list at
https://mailchi.mp/ee42ccbc6409/zoeburtonsignup

~Zoe

About the Author

Zoe Burton first fell in love with Jane Austen's books in 2010, after seeing the 2005 version of Pride and Prejudice on television. While making her purchases of Miss Austen's novels, she discovered Jane Austen Fan Fiction; soon after that she found websites full of JAFF. Her life has never been the same. She began writing her own stories when she ran out of new ones to read.

Zoe lives in a 100-plus-year-old house in the snow-belt of Ohio with her Boxer, Jasper. She is a former Special Education Teacher, and has a passion for romance in general, *Pride and Prejudice* in particular, and stock car racing.

Connect with Zoe Burton

Email:

zoe@zoeburton.com

Facebook:

https://www.facebook.com/ZoeBurtonBooks

https://www.facebook.com/groups/BurtonsBabes/

Website:

https://zoeburton.com

Support me at Patreon:

https://www.patreon.com/zoeburtonauthor

Join my mailing list:

https://mailchi.mp/ee42ccbc6409/zoeburtonsignup

Pinterest:

https://www.pinterest.com/zoeburtonauthor

More by Zoe Burton

Regency Single Titles:

I Promise To...

Lilacs & Lavender

Promises Kept

Bits of Ribbon and Lace

Decisions and Consequences

Mr. Darcy's Love

Darcy's Deal

The Essence of Love

Matches Made at Netherfield

Darcy's Perfect Present

Darcy's Surprise Betrothal

To Save Elizabeth

Darcy Overhears

Merry Christmas, Mr. Darcy!

Darcy's Secret Marriage

Darcy's Christmas Compromise

Darcy's Predicament

Darcy's Uneasy Betrothal

Darcy's Yuletide Wedding

Darcy's Unwanted Bride

Darcy's Favorite

Darcy's Christmas Scheme

Mr. Darcy: The Key to Her Heart

Victorian Romance:

A MUCH Later Meeting

WESTERN ROMANCE:

Darcy's Bodie Mine

Bundles:

Promises

The Darcy Marriage Series Books 1-3

Christmas in Meryton

The Darcy Marriage Series:

Darcy's Wife Search

Lady Catherine Impedes

Caroline's Censure

In Peril with Darcy Series:

Darcy's Happy Compromise

Darcy's Honorable Proposal

Pride & Prejudice & Racecars

Darcy's Race to Love

Georgie's Redemption

Darcy's Caution